I0681111

8th House Publishing
Montreal, Canada
www.8thHousePublishing.com

Published in Canada by 8thHousePublishing.

Cover Design by 8th House Publishing.
Cover Artwork by Rachael Alice Parsons

A CIP catalogue record for this book is available from Library
and Archives Canada.

LIBRARY AND ARCHIVES CANADA
CATALOGUING IN PUBLICATION
Unwanted Hopeless Romantic Morons / Parsons, Geoffrey
Alexander (1981 -)

ISBN 978-0-9809108-9-6 (pb)

1. Literature--Fiction. I. Title

8th House Publishing
Montreal, Canada

Unwanted Hopeless Romantic Morons

by

Geoffrey Alexander Parsons

CONTENTS

Unwanted Hopeless Romantic Morons

An Unwanted Email

AFTER I WROTE YOU that last email I went and drank on top of the Vs, then did some coke, then lost my bank card and went to the bank on Saturday all cracked out and demanded to get a new card so I could "get my fucking money out of the bank! I give you my fucking business don't I!? Well I want my fucking money that I earned. I could come in here with crack pipe fucking burns all over my face and I should still get my FUCKING money!!!" (I only snort coke but I was making a deluded point). Then one of the friends I got fucked up with (I paid for everything) calls me at 2 am last night and says, "Well, I am not blaming you but I got a fucked up knee from wrestling with you. They had to drain the blood." I said that was too bad, and did he have any money to pay me back and he should give me more of his valiums. He said he would, but his roommate had to come out. They were both extremely drunk... When I got back to my house I realized it was 2 am and became pissed, so I called him back and told him that I never wanted to hear from him or any of the people that are associated with him ever again in his pathetic life... I used the word 'cunt' profusely... Then I took the valium and tried to go to sleep, ringing my hands and angry: shaking with anger. At work the next day, the girl I have the huge fucking crush on was ignoring me. I kept trying to talk to her, small talk, not too much, like, 'How are you doing today? How about the weather?'

She was acting obviously pissed, so I asked her: "What is up? Are you in a bad mood?" and she said, "Yes, I am having a bad day like you have sometimes."

"Look is this about me not talking to you on Friday?"

"Yes," she said. "You are acting like a baby. You want to work with me all the time." (We work in the same room.)

"I think *you* are acting like a baby," I said. "I asked you to help me with a toy order that came in and you said okay. I asked you like, three times."

"Oh, I was working all day," she said, like I wasn't or something. In fact, Kim, I work harder than anyone else in the whole fucking building!

"Fine," I said. "I won't talk to you ever again then."

"You say that..." she started, but I left the room. I was so angry I was about to quit. And I still think this girl is great? What the fuck? Am I so fucking guilty about my own "bad" behaviour that I allow myself to be a victim of people that care nothing for me? Why do I care about this girl that cares nothing for me? Why do I feel like crying all the time? Why do my moods change every two minutes? Why do I tell you? Why do I want to keep relationships with people like you that have driven me to emotional breakdowns? Why do I think that I can be saved by people that hate me? This girl does not know the bad things I do. She knows nothing of it. She dislikes me because I like her so much and she is afraid of being hurt. So fuck her, right? But this sucks: I have to work with her every day. When I see her I want to cry. I think she laughs about it behind my back.

OH, AND AT THE BANK I made a scene and security was called and I fought the two of them. I was doing an okay job: they were smacking my head on the ground and I was yelling, "I just want to take money from my bank! People, I implore you!" Then the cops came. They pepper-sprayed me, but I still kept yelling at them and cursing at them, using 'cunt' as much as possible. My new favourite swear word... Then at the cop shop they bashed my head against the floor until my face started to bleed and I started sobbing, "Please stop! I am sorry. You win, you are the boss. I am shit. Don't hurt me, please." All the cops were cheering the guy on: "Get some blood Bratser! Kick his ass!" Then in the cell I yelled over and over about what injustices they had done, and how I would sue their pig pants off, and how I should not be afraid of people that are supposed to be out there to help people, not to arrest people that try to take their own money from the bank...

No charges were laid. Anyway, Kim: After Christmas, I am going back to Halifax. I am a mess. I am on the verge of killing myself. I am weak. I have a hard time smiling, and I think it would be a good idea if you do not talk to me or email me when I get back. I am a bad fucking guy, a shit, a fuck up. I might hate women, even though I do not want to. Really, I feel like nothing and dead and I know my parents will help me a bit when I get back. And if not, I know some people there that won't turn me down if I quit drinking which I am trying to do. I don't think I can live through another Christmas on the bottle. Last one, I got a gnawing ulcer. But Kim, I like you. You are a good girl but don't fucking get in touch with me after Christmas because I am afraid that history will repeat itself.

Anyway, that is how things are going with me. My karma is all fucked up. I thought I was due for some good but I am just getting bombarded with pain and suffering. I tried to make my self-loathing and misogyny as entertainingly as possible. This was all true, Kim. I feel very unsafe here. I am going home because I feel alone and in danger here. It is crazy and I am crazy. *There* is my soul right under the mustard stain on my sleeve.

And since you liked it sooo much last time I wrote it, *ta ta*

TOM

Life's Façade

NOTHING IS UNBEARABLE. Something would be bearable, though. Entertaining. Scattered describes the room nice-like. Used condoms and Mr. Noodle packs. The smell of classless clean. Like the smell of a just-vacuumed hick's home, shampooed deer antlers and all. Summer rain is a welcome change to what had become a daunting killer stagnant heat. A black woman scolds her children in a harsh and endearing way. And, as the façade of life goes on, nobody notices, and if you make any comment, you'd be told to mind your business, to which you could reply: Mind your own because it is my business whose business I mind. Then you'd be shut down with: Treat others the way you'd like to be treated.

NOT A WORD IS SPOKEN but there is a silent discourse between my associate and me. As he flicks the channel between CNN and FOX News to watch the coverage on a dead pedophile that no one would have suspected 'til his death when someone read his diary and told the world. A senator, this man was a Republican, and one of the unnecessary evils that plague the Earth.

My associate slaps his cardac pants. He takes a sip of Jack Daniels and we do a line of coke that has the taste of mint to it.

"So what is it today?" he asks.

"Give me a swig."

My associate hands me the bottle and I drink it down. "Well, there's a fire in me today, friend. Scum of the earth like this running the country! Only thing to do is go on some kind of a spree."

"Indeed." He's hoarse, but his voice

still deep, rich.

THE BUICK CHUGS UP like a morning shower loogie and rips along the rain beading on the window being smacked off like cum off a cock at midnight in Las Vegas. Roll down those bloody memories like sun-faded bright vivid colors. Through my mind run thoughts of getting to the casino and winning the jackpot.

"A big win is waiting down at the center there."

I say this in telepathic to my associate whom I hate and would sell out to the police later on. Numerous trafficking charges, of course, because I have the tapes.

The casino entrance is veiled in hookers with tight red booty shorts. We wade through with slight erections due to the sluts fondling their breasts and pursing their lips. The only thing saving me from a full-blown hard-on is the thought of their green mucus-filled snatches.

Inside we use magnetic devices, handcrafted by my associate to trip the slot machines and win a considerable sum, a suite, and our choice of the casino's finest whores. I pick Mandy who boasts that she can suck a cock so good that my penis will be rendered dysfunctional for hours, but not to worry because she'll stick around and snort blow till I am ready to fuck her vigorously, high as fuck.

"You'll like it," she whispers in my ear, groping for my cock.

Sirens scream out at noon and Mandy has left. Hotel officials had to come up and take her out on a stretcher. I am an epileptic seizer. At least she and I had finished our business. It is Monday, so to work I stumble off after picking up a prescription of Benzos at the pharmacy.

THE AD AGENCY IS A GREY SHIT-LOG in the toilet bowl city. I pop a Benzo and duck into the café below. I give a sheepish smile to the woman with freckles and large tits who serves the coffee. She knows the routine: By mid-week, I'll be flirtatious, but Monday I am always blazé. I feel like saying something like, 'you have a marvelous rack miss'. But I don't have the guts... White-walled office and the eyes of twelve or so smiled-up cunts of men in ties and fresh suits and coffees in hand. The boss throws me a grapefruit.

"Okay Tom, this is what we're working on."

I smile. Grapefruits. An easy vegetable to sell to the peons. I'll give a call to my friends in the food guide department.

"I'll make it sexy," I say.

"Just what I like to hear, Tom."

"I'll have to take some days in the field..."

"Oh of course, Tom. I figured that much."

"Can I hold on to this grapefruit?" I ask.

"Of course, Tom. It's yours."

The office all look with their envious leers and glares.

NOTHING IS UNBEARABLE. Work is too easy. Life is given to me, handed to me on a silver platter, if you will, this façade of a life a caring individual. BULLSHIT rules the world. Don't tell me it's love. Maybe if love was hate. Hate is love. Nothing is unbearable.

I made a TV commercial with a model and a grapefruit dancing around. 'Because it's good for you' was the end tag. Then people break-dancing. I got a raise. I am done in this void. Money is life. Life is money.

ONLY GENIUSES GO TO THE LIBRARY

I WENT TO THE LIBRARY around 9:30 AM to use the computers. They give out a free hour of time to people. I run into a buddy there. Jason is his name. He has his hair bleached blond. All we ever do is drink whiskey and walk around talking about chicks and trying to mac on them. I wake up in the morning, perhaps in the drunk tank, with eight girl's phone numbers and email addresses... Today is Halloween. This calls for whiskey and to go to the mall and drink it mixed with A&W root beer or coke. We sit out on the patio.

"Hey there sweetness," Jason says to a girl walking by, and she returns an embarrassed smile. We both give her our respective sex eyes.

"What are you up to? That shirt looks good on you. You know that?" I say lighting a smoke, and wink.

I am wearing a green blazer. I have a cabby hat pulled to the side. It is 12:30 PM and we are starting on our first pints of whiskey for the day. We look like the hoodlums of any generation...

"Thanks, but I got to go," says the girl.

I ask for her number... I get her name: it's Candice.

Later on we are walking around. The crew is getting bigger and bigger. We go to a graveyard to drink. I tell everyone that if we sit on the graves we'll steal the life force of that person. They call me strange and sit on them.

Then I can't really remember... I woke up in the drunk tank with a shit load of phone numbers. I was angry. I told the cops I didn't respect them and kicked over their garbage can.

"Why don't you pick up the fucking drug dealer and meth heads? and crack heads?"

They told me to pick up the garbage lid, which I did, giving them the finger as I walked out the door, a rage surging through me like fucking fire ripping through a rain forest. I went home and slept.

FRAGMENTS
(The Midget and the Giant)

SNOW FELL EARLY that December morning, but it was a sunny snow: light flakes, just floating around in the air, and if you looked up it would dance in your vision for hours. The tall buildings were just visible over the tree line, something that some people disliked, but Randal loved it. It was where the city met the forest. It was the last vestige of hope, it was balance, he thought, in a way.

Standing at six seven, Randal was somewhat of an oddity, even in this day and age. He would have been looked down on if that were possible. (ha ha!)

He had frizzed mad scientist hair. He also had a list of people to kill he kept with him from when he was a child. He also had never had a girlfriend and was twenty-five years old.

Randal was standing at the edge of the city in the first snowfall on a December morning. Chuck was a round, short chubby Chuck. A little brawler when he got a little too inebriated, but usually a fairly tame and sensitive guy. Sensitivity was required to be around Randolph, who got offended easily. They had a bottle of whiskey and were talking.

"What are we doing here, you know? Out here in the woods drinking a bottle of fucking whiskey! My mother was a university professor, my father a lawyer and I am what?"

"A working class schmuck," said Chuck with a half grin, because he was too, and because he knew it was no joke. Because he knew that song by John Lennon was a lie, and heroes don't mean anything. And heroes don't get nothing, not that either of them were heroes. Neither of them had saved a baby from a burning building or saved a drowning elderly woman that had slipped off a dock or any shit like that. But they were working class: a construction worker and a cook at a shitty restaurant that made bar food, exclusively.

"Yaaa, well... fuck. I don't want this. I want something more."

"We all do, I think. And those that say they don't, well, fuck they are fucking lying."

"Yup," Randal said and picked up a rock and flung it at a tree, a pine tree, and there was a bit of snow on it that sprayed off from the branches. He smiled and turned to Chuck who was staring off to the side, and his overbite was sadly exposed. Poor Chuck, Randal thought.

They walked along the path and saw some kids walking along in fur jackets and the guys were in just parkas, not fur. It was a group of four or five guys and two girls. They were all laughing. As they walked by Randal and Chuck, the girls giggled and Chuck turned and smiled at them. Randal slapped him on the back.

Randal thought it was pointless, and they were not in the slightest bit interested in them, and he was probably right.

Chuck's smiling pissed off one of the guys, a blond-haired guy, six foot one, perfect teeth, and a crew cut. He wore a bomber jacket.

"The fuck you looking at, freak?" he yelled at Chuck.

Chuck smiled. "That's a beautiful girl there... you have."

Chuck walked over to Randal's and everyone's surprise. He just bang kissed one of the brunette girls on the lips that looked so nice and plump cherry red. She didn't push him away. She grabbed his jacket (Chuck's) and pulled herself towards him thrusting out her pelvis. This didn't go over well with the perfect boys.

"Sally what the fuck you's doing? Buddy what you do to her?"

It was strange. The girl looked transfixed and by no means was Chuck that good looking; he was not really even *kind* of good looking. No girl to Randal's recollection had even spoken to Chuck. Chuck told the girl to stand aside a moment and walked up to the guy and smacked him in the jaw, a right hook, as fast as can be and the guy dropped just like that. Randal and Chuck then started to run down the snowy path back to the city.

"Fucking moron! Those were like fucking high-school kids!"

"They have to learn."

They were both starting to gasp. No one was following them. The friends of the guy that was knocked out looked scared when they left. The path on the way out had that kind of snow that has like ice shell over softer snow under the shell. There was a path through the trees and a smaller foot path big enough for one person. Pine trees were all around.

"It is beginning to feel a lot like Christmas." Chuck said. His breathing was not so much gasping anymore.

Randal smiled down at Chuck. "Fucking dick," he said. "You're such a prick, man what'd you have to go and do that for. They were just kids!"

"They were asking for it..."

"They were fucking kids. And what was that kiss about?" Randal's voice took on a bit of an awed sounding questioning tone, thingamajigger type of tone, you know?

"It was nothing," Chuck said, and they both went to their homes.

COPS SHOWED UP at Chuck's door. Chuck knew the cops, all of them, and they knew him. "Hello!" Chuck said with a cheerful tone. "Nice day today, you don't think?" It was doing the same sun snow thing.

"Chuck..." It was officer MacDougal, a particularly large and snarly police officer, and one that had little respect for anyone he talked to but his fellow officers. "You and that giant friend of yours, what's your freak friend's name again?" MacDougal smiled down at Chuck (as everyone did and had too). "You two were out for a stroll yesterday around three in the afternoon?" He gave a cynical smirk. This cop was your regular wise-ass coffee swilling black-and-white seeing shithead.

"What, you calling me and Randal gay?

Well maybe we are! This is harassment!"

MacDougal looked back at his fellow officer, and smiled. Chuck was using a fake lisp. He was over-doing it, hand limp at the wrist, smacking it off his cheeks and thigh, just whacking it all around his body. Anyone but MacDougal would've thought that Chuck was a mad man.

"Chuck that kid you smacked was only fucking sixteen years old. When you going to wise up? Now the kid was saying nothing but I knew it was you two fuck-ups. Seen you up there too many times. Grow the fuck up!"

MacDougal always gave this speech when he could not prove something. MacDougal left.

"So MacDougal came by."

"Oh yeah?" Randal was on the phone. He had been masturbating when the phone rang. Chucks voice put him down. The mention of MacDougal buried him.

METH HEAD GIRL

IT IS FALL. I am sitting with an 18 year old girl on the steps of a church across from MacDonald's. We are sharing a cheeseburger. It is damp outside and the streets look cold and unforgiving. Even the golden arches look sinister in the mood of the street—a shame and a reality.

"You know what I think the best part of getting high is?" asks the girl in her customary spaced-out way.

"No," I say with a trying sympathetic tone. "I don't get high, really."

"Well it's *not* the not eating. And it's *not* the not sleeping. I love both of that stuff..." She looks at me and smiles. I smile back. "It is the act of it. The smoking of it."

"Don't do it too much," I say. "Puts holes in your brain."

"Lots of things put holes in your brain," she outlandishly offers. "Everyone is so dead set against meth." This in a sarcastic mockery of these people who think crystal meth is an evil. I am one of these people; I am being mocked.

But I tell her: "I was talking to a guy that was a meth head for a long time and he said that he found it hard to talk and shit after he quit—said that his brain started to liquidize or something like that." She offers me some cheeseburger. I take some.

"Ever wonder why they call it Jib?" she asks. She thinks she's schooling me.

"Because if you do it long enough you only talk gibberish?"

"Yah."

We sit watching the mist of the night come across the park. I blow my nose into a napkin and she nestles her head into my chest. I am thinking the whole time what a sad scene, what a sad state of affairs. And the more you dissect and plunge into the depths of the situation, the more sad and daunting and mocking and rabid it becomes, gnawing and tearing the city to shreds and turning a generation into a hopped up bunch of dead-at-25's.

GOING TO THE MOVIES

SCENE I

IT IS RAINING and the wind is blowing the trees around and large streams of water are coming off the leaves. A woman with blond hair and a golden plastic crown and a white bridesmaid's dress walks along the street. She smiles at a man on the side of the street in an inlet of a storefront. The man is in an army fatigue jacket and has a down mohawk and a nose ring. He smiles back. The woman stops to light a smoke.

Woman:

"Do you have a light?"

Her voice is strong and cuts through the sound of the strong blowing winds.

Man
(in badly faked English accent):
"Yes m'lady."

Woman
(in a fine, faked English accent):
"Why thank you sir."

The man holds out a Bic and lights it. The flame goes out in the wind. The woman draws nearer until they are almost touching. Together they make a shield with their bodies against the howling winds. Her smoke is lit and she takes a long drag and exhales as if in ecstasy. The man stands in awe like there is some special life force, something emanating from her, some power greater than his cognitive ability to understand. She walks on leaving the man awestruck for several moments. Then the man goes into his bag and pulls out a pipe and drops in a rock and lights his rock.

Through the night, the man walks with a large garbage bag filled to the max. He walks around, his jacket opening up and blowing to the side. His down mohawk is all askew. He walks up the steps to a church and the door opens. His face is covered with the warm, engrossing light.

The women walks on, smoking her cigarette with orgasmic pleasure. There are 'Happy Halloween' posters all over and skeletons and pumpkins, ghouls and the like. Every now and then, a small figure draped in a bed sheet scampers by. She is in a residential neighbourhood with an unlit smoke. She stops and walks up the iron spiral stairwell into a very well-to-do prim-proper home and opens the door.

SCENE II

In the front room of a dark house is the

sound of the rain falling on the roof. She turns off the light and her smile fades in to a smirk. She fiddles around in her purse and produces a bag of white powder and puts it on the table. Then another. She sits down in the wooden chair—an antique. She smiles and then rage fills her eyes. Her face reddens, eyes as intense as comets flying through the vacuum of space, going nowhere, lost. She spots some coke on the table and divvies herself up a huge line. Snorts it with a hundred dollar bill.

SCENE III

Red leaves on the ground and orange in the trees. The man walks along the street with another man, this one slightly younger with a large cut along his forehead. He wears plaid pants.

Steve:

"Chuck, man, you should've seen this girl last night that came up to me at the spot."

Chuck:
(Cutting in, his voice is rough as though it is weather-beaten.)
"You fuck her?"

Steve:
"No, I just lit her smoke."

Steve stares off in a trance and a strange inhuman grin begins to develop on his face.

Chuck:
"Well, she musta been something,"

Looking at Steve without understanding. Shaking his head.

Chuck:
"I light people's smokes all the fucking time, Steve-o. That is no biggie. She did not give you a little suckasucky or nothing?"

Steve stops dead in his tracks. He looks into his pocket and produces a 100 dollar bill.

Steve:
"She must have been high. I snagged this," he says placidly.

Chuck:
"Well then, my brother, let's get high."

The two walk off around a brick building. The leaves falling in the forefront like snowflakes. A Porsche drives by the exact place they had left, stops, and a man gets out in a pinstriped suit. He is holding a briefcase. He walks in to the office building. A bird lands before his feet and instead of moving or avoiding the bird the man steps right on it, then looking down he smiles, dashes his shoe off in a puddle. The puddle fills with blood as we fade out...

SCENE IV

A soup kitchen, yellow linoleum floors, yellow walls covered with grey and brown marks, the low mumble of sixty or so old homeless men. A turkey dinner sits in front of Steve. He is in a parka that is open to reveal a dirty white t-shirt. He forks the turkey in a forlorn way. Over the loud speaker is Christmas music which makes for a dreary effect given the surroundings, a mocking, almost. Steve's grim smirk is growing as his nostrils are flaring up as if he smells something putrid. He looks over his shoulder and scratches his head.

Steve:
"Fuck!"

He stands up. The crowd of homeless rejects are all looking at him. A plate smashes on the floor. It is over in a moment. Steve is breathing heavily and intensely staring at the turkey on the paper plate in front of him.

An old man:
"Eat it up, boy!"

Steve has seen him before. He wears a poppy. He always wears a poppy.

Steve:
"Well how can you be so content with this?"

The old man smiles an old codger's enchanting whimsical smile and pats his chest.

The old man:
"I got the lord in here."

Steve:
"Oh yeah, of course. So you don't mind the shit and the puke and the piss? The looks from people, the fucking music?"

(shouting)
"The FUCKING MUSIC...?"

Two men from the mission in blue shirts and buzz cuts, holding walkie-talkies approach.

Security Guard 1:
"You have to leave sir."

They each grab one of his arms.
Steve:
"Oh you're going to fucking escort me out. You fucking pricks! Where do you stay? What's your life?"

Security Guard 2:
"We are doing our best to help and then... Then there are little shits like you."

They take Steve out without another peep out of him, throw him out into a dark alleyway by the back exit and leave him.

Steve looks around surging with anger, breathing heavily. His chest is heaving. A snickerer's grin on his lips, bubbles of snot coming out his nose. He fiddles around his parka jacket. He keeps looking as we lift up from him into the night to the roof tops.

SCENE V

A bowl of coke sits in the middle of the table. There is a man and the woman from the street. She is in a blue dress and she looks amazing. An angel, quite. She is sitting, staring at the man who is quite older and dressed impeccably in the highest of fucking yuppie styles. He smiles. Or tries to, but no matter how many time he tries all he can manage is a hint of a smile at the corner of his mouth.

The man:
"Jane, you look wonderful."

Jane (smiles):
"Thank you, Don. You don't look that bad yourself."

She sticks her fingernail in the bowl of coke that is acting as cornucopia and snorts it.

She flings her blonde hair back.
"Don, you sure know how to treat a
lady."

Don:
(with the smile he has finally managed)
"You're not a lady, Jane, you know that.
Now come over here."

*Startled by his remark Jane works the
smile back onto her face and comes across
the table lifting her dress exposing a garter
and white stockings.*

Jane:
"Happy Thanksgiving. Ha ha. You got
a lot to be thankful about with me here
baby."

Don:
"You're a bag a dozen baby,"

*He pulls her off the table and she straddles
his crotch.*
He smacks her across the face.

Don:

"Jane, are you a good girl?"

Jane:
(with a shudder in her voice)
"No Daddy, I am bad. I am a bad little girl."

Don smacks her again and kisses her. He pulls her panties down to her thighs as she unbuttons his pants and then this smacking sound "smack smack smack" to fade out to black smacking sounds turn to the beat of a song...

On the hustling streets, rain is falling in large pools and cars splatter men in hats with ear flaps. Zoom out from a man getting completely soaked from head to toe to inside where Jane and her sister sit. Her sister has brown hair and eyes, somewhat more homely looking in comparison with Jane's angelic looks.

Jane:
(in mid conversation):
"Yeah, so his dick had this weird slant to it, like to the left kinda."

Jane sticks out her finger to the right.

Her sister:
"That is the right."

Jane:
(laughing)
"To you it ain't."

Her sister:
(not seeing the humor in the comment)
"Yeah. Aw, Jane, so what have you been
up to? Mom and dad are worried. And
don't think I can't see that shiner under
your foundation there, you bitch."

Jane:
(off-handed)
"Well, you know how I like it."

Jane's sister:
"I know, but I don't know why. What do
you get out of it aside from coke?"

Jane:
(putting her hand on the crotch of a

waiter walking by and squeezing)
"Hello Sailor!"

The waiter looks down with an uncontrollable smile.

Waiter:
(surprisingly calm under pressure)
"What will it be ma'am?"

Jane:
"Hamburger with cheese."

Jane's sister:
(disgusted)
"The same."

The waiter leaves with a bit of a tent in the crotch area. Jane and her sister sit. Jane's sister looks astonished. Jane's face has a too-cool look on it. She has always been the cool one.

Jane:
"Have you ever been smacked real hard? And have a big cock in you at the same time?"

Jane's sister:
"No."

Jane (smiling):
"Well, shut up then."

Jane's sister gets up and walks out. Jane sits with an indistinguishable smile on her face. The waiter comes back with the cheeseburger. She looks up at him with a smile.

Jane:
"When you get off?"

Waiter:
"Uh, what do you mean?"

Jane:
"Well, you want a fuck or what?"

SCENE VI

Rain falling outside. Sweeping shot of street of old men with ear flaps get soaked by passing SUVs. Bag ladies and guys in sunglasses, out-of-everyone's-league girls with Dior sunglasses float by on the air, putting it on. Darkness.

SCENE VII

Morning sunshine in the drying streets, country music somewhere in the background. Right in front of a garage sits Steve, smoking a cigarette. A fat man in a track suit walks up: Fubu. He is white. Irish most likely, red hair. He stops in front of Steve for a moment and then walks off. Moments later, Steve walks off in the opposite direction.

In an alley way Steve and his buddy sit, a new buddy.

Steve:
"So this shit is okay."

New buddy:
"Yeah, it's good. I am fucking high."

Steve:
"Yeah, this is the life."

The dark alleyway is moving with small rodents, suggestive squeaks, and rummaging. The pitter-patter of rain starts up like a car starting. Tin-tin on some tin roof.

New buddy:
"Did I ever tell you that I have a wife and kids back home. They kicked me to the curb. She didn't know, you know, and she caught me and some pals cooking up in the kitchen."

The new buddy has no expression. He looks off into a void that he and only he knows. The rain keeps falling making puddles. Time lapse of them sitting or squatting in the alley way doing bowls and looking straight forwards as the puddles fill up and little rings fly out from drops.

Steve:
"Well, I am off."

He gets up and leaves his new, recently, just recently old buddy alone in his personal abyss.

Following Steve along the street, it looks unforgiving. The rain whispers discouragements to Steve, which shows on his sorrowful face as he walks along soaked. Some sad Radiohead song or something lightly plays under the rain drops. Real tear jerking shit. If you can feel for a person like that.

SCENE VIII

A nice house. Nice in that it is clean. Occupants are normal people with half-

decent jobs each, a couple in their 50s, healthy. They are sitting at a strong looking table made of wood, impeccably varnished. The woman has a northern Ontario biddy drawl to her.

Woman:
"I saw that kid around the store again. I wish he could clean himself up."

Christmas songs play in the background, Frank Sinatra crooning his ass off. The music is there as much as if you could see Sinatra swaggering and cocking his ego laden head around in the way cool guys do.

Man:
(with that New York, but not from New York, tough-guy talk.)

"Well, people make their own choices, don't they, May? The kid should be locked up, that would get him out of everyone's garbage. Sitting there on the side of the street, does the kid have no fucking respect?"

"…Anyway May, don't think about him,
that is how the terrorists win."

Woman:
"You think he is a terrorist?"

Man:
"Of some kind, May, of some kind."

*Sinatra still singing delightfully in the
background. You can almost smell the
cookies as May pulls them out of the oven.*

SCENE IX

*Jane is dressed to the nines. She is walking
down a done up Christmas Blvd and
smiling. Men stop and smile. Catcalls are
being yelled. She grabs her breast and makes
a lewd gesture to appease the pervs as they
ogle.*

Red shoes, by Tom Waits is blasting as she walks in to a record store, her red high heels walking in to the beat. It is sex and sexy and sordid all at the same time. She stops at the counter folding her arms over the top of the register on her tippy toes.

Jane:
"Hey sis."

Jane's sister:
(looking up, dazed)
"Jane? What's up? What you doing up so early?"

Jane:
"Late nights turn into early mornings pretty quick."

You can tell she's high from her sheepish smile. In the light, one can see her makeup coming into that cracked cake kind of layered look.

Jane:
"Why you listen to this guy? His voice is horrible…"

Jane's sister:
"I don't really want you here."

SCENE X

A man stands on the well kept lawn. Jack
walks up a gravel path towards him.

Smiling man:
"Glad you came Jack."

Jack and the man walk in to the gray tall
building.

Inside the building are linoleum floors and
many rooms. The man introduces himself
as Mr. Brown.

Mr. Brown
(to a man sitting a white desk with
phone):
"I love to see them come young."

(Series of shots)

1.   Jack clean shaven waking up in a clean white sheeted bed.

2.   A room full of men and women in a dark basement. A man stands up and says, "My name is Rick and I am an addict."

3.   Jack running in a field with vibrant green grass.

4.   Jack walking out of a high rise building, swinging his jacket over his shoulder.

5.   Jack walks in to a basement with a bunch of people sitting in chairs. AA slogans writing all around. Reverse zoom out from Jack's smiling face.

SCENE XI

A girl stands on the corner. Blood is streaming from her face. Camera moves in: slowly realize that is is Jane.

A man walks by.

Jane:
"Please help me sir!! Waaaa!"

Jane lunges for the man. He walks off into the street to avoid her.

 Cut to—Jack walking down the street in nice clean clothing. There are lots of dirty men and women in the back and foreground, shopping carts and cardboard homes. Jack stops by a younger looking guy with a buzz cut smoking some type of rolled cigarette.

Jack:
"What happened to that women down there?"

Man:
(smoking a joint)
"The girl with blood all over her
screaming like a banshee?"

(laughs)

Jack gives a judging glance and smiles.

Jack:
"Yeah, the crazy bloody banshee."

Man:
"Yeah she owed a dealer. She got bear
maced and smacked in the face. I don't
know how much she owed, but she's
lucky."

*Jack shakes his head and pulls out his cell
phone.*

Jack:
"Hi, I am calling in an emergency."

*The ambulance arrives and collects the
woman. Her eyes open and close, then open
and the scene slowly comes into focus and*

Jack is sitting in the hospital with a smile on his face.

Fade to white

FIN

THE GIRL FRIEND

I WALK INTO THE BASEMENT apartment through the courtyard. The plateau in winter is as beautiful as in spring or summer or fall. There is my girl in the kitchen making something, cutting the garlic. I have a beer from the corner store. She is not happy about this fact.

"Tom, why did you have to do that?"

"It's *one* beer and I just got off work."

"Yeah, but it's never just one beer with you."

"Okay, don't be a bitch," I say, cracking the beer. I feel bad. I put the feeling out with beer.

"I am not being a bitch Tom and I wish you would not keep calling me one," she says. She is angry, but not that angry. I know that I could say a few more rude things to her and still be able to have sex with her a couple times.

"Let's go to the bar tonight. Call up one of your girl friends. I bet Laura's doing something."

"Laura hates you, Tom."

"Well, she's a bitch anyway."

"You only say that because you'll never be able to fuck her."

"I love you."

"Tom, you don't know what love is." She is cutting her garlic with some rage now.

"Simmer with the chopping you crazy girl," I say and give a cute smile. I know it is cute because she has told me it is. She laughs over her garlic and then laughs some more. The laughing gets to the point where it scares me a bit. A minute later, she starts crying. She accidentally cuts herself with the knife. The blood flows, sprays. I set down my beer and go over to her and grab her arms.

"Let go of me! You abuse me, Tom! You're cutting me! You are such an asshole, you know!"

"Are you going to cut yourself again?"

"No." And I believe her. I need a walk. I am steaming. This cutting… It bothers me. It's nippy outside and the wind hits my face. I feel like crying. Snow is swept along the road and it looks like crystals and diamonds dancing and tumbling down the street. I buy another beer and find an alleyway and sit there and drink. The warming effect of the beer and the snowy night hit the romantic strings in my soul and I think of her, my girlfriend, in the warm glow of the apartment making up a meal, bleeding and crying. I finish the beer and go back to the house. And there she is and it's alright.

Later, we go out. Her friends are all against me, I have figured out. We play pool and I am in a good groove. I am cocky and slick my hair back in the washroom so I look like a goofy-faced James Dean or something, a smoke hanging out the side of my mouth and a swagger that makes my girl smile and her friends cringe. We do lines in the bathroom. It's all good and fun again.

THE ALIENS ARE ATTACKING

SITTING THERE ON THE COUCH, in a room my brother would say smells too much like cock... "Too much cock around there," my brother told me about the Bartins' place. I moved in above their place with Franklin, my buddy from back in school. They were all my friends from back in school, and I was enjoying being the new kid in town again after being away.

I had a little band going that sucked, of course. I was even keeping my drinking to a somewhat respectable level. But the reason I had come back was to destroy the very fiber of the very light scene of a throw blanket which will be called 'Hopeless Regression into Old Love'. First love, at that. I might as well have tried to crawl back into the womb.

I'll just let that point go off to nowhere at all, let it stand there in its shit encrusted sandy foundation and move along to the "BAND MAN!" Right now it is Christmas 2006, but this was around Christmas 2005. Things have changed but at that time a man by the name of Pette had a house hidden out on the highway. In his attic, he had a little recording studio. My brother and a couple of other guys would go up there and jam with the guitars and bass, and pretend we weren't feeling like a bunch of silly fuckers.

The songs we had were filthy grunger throw backs and we would track stuff, then do a track-over of us all yelling and screaming and add reverb and digital delay so it end up sounding so mucky that we'd all try and pawn it off as nothing, nothing serious.

Nothing serious: like Pette and his alien research that he would do late at night while his girlfriend worked all day. For Pette was on unemployment after "working his ass off for years" as he put it.

"Oh, they're out there, Tom. Why is that so crazy?" Pette would say, imploring me to agree.

"It is not that crazy, Pette. I just think it takes away from better thoughts."

I cleared my throat and looked back in my brain to find the proper and fitting words. "It's like you need to believe in that to get to sleep at night or something..."

"Oh," he says. And I have upset Pette; he puts his hand up to stop me from even venturing to apologize. "And you don't do the same thing with booze? We all need to escape and get away from the stresses of day to day life."

"But why fucking aliens?"

"Well I found this site in my surfing last night: a man that worked for the CIA and the FBI. It is kind of top secret. I am getting kind of paranoid about it."

Pette starts to shake a bit, then he yells: "Cunts!" in a strained old man voice and I laugh my ass off as does my brother.

"Okay, let's get jamming then," I say, and pick up the bass and we went to 'er.

STRANGE SEEDS
(Dead at 25s)

"TOM, WHAT YOU UP TO?"

There it was, Slak's jackass face, looking right at me with all its scar tissue.

"Nothing, Slak, to work: telemarketing."

I met Slak on the street. Back when I still enjoyed getting drunk everyday and being dirty, and bumming change. Slak looks different now too, cleaner, and he has fewer cuts on his face. Still lots of scars though. I was feeling kind of bored so I continued on with our conversation.

"So, Slak, what you up to lately? 'spearing change for drinking beer and kicking ass'?"

That was the slogan back in the day, back last summer.

He said no, and he was telemarketing now, too. Telemarketing is not such a transition from bumming change really. Bumming change is probably more dignified! Slak said he *really* had to go, as though he didn't want to hurt whatever feelings he thought I had to be hurt. I am flying right past telemarketing. Fuck it! It's for dimwitted fools! Stuck up image is everything; dicks and whores. People that talk about reality TV shows and clothing. But me, I am going to crack open some mother-fucking insane ass trip for you all, that college and university professors won't like. It's a whole lot more real than anything dipped in grease in the white house kitchen!

September 29

I took a day off work to drink. The

hurricane was coming through Montreal, or the remnants of it. I thought it would be a nice day to hide in my room and drink, but by the third or fourth beer I decided to go down the park with the statue of the French man that lost his hat. There I would start my show. Weather affects me just as it does dogs, or birds.

A couple of bums were around, 50 years old or so. Fat, all of them, with dirty ball caps and 40's of beer. My friends and audience and players on the stage of my intoxication show, which some love and others hate. The bum with the gesture was saying that he was cold so I gave him my hoody. He sauntered off, or more like wobbled.

A conversation with a couple of university girls: I was squatting in front of their bench. They asked what I was doing in the park that day, and I told them that I was hitting on them, and they asked, "Both of us?" I said yes, and then they said, "Our boyfriends will love that!"

Oh and the show must go on—I must

be satisfied!

Later I am drinking with some street punks, and one of them pulls out some seeds and makes a tea. Says if I can drink the whole thing and the seeds in the bottom, I can have the last beer. I do. The show gets blurry — staggering around — no balance. And then a hospital. They had me in restraints. I screamed. And they let me out.

September 30— Payday
I puked in the parking lot behind work, no food, just beer. It's pretty sick. I am saying to myself, "I need a beer to calm my nerves." The manager came in. I find out I am only getting paid 149.00 for the week I had 14 sales on the board, they are all bad. I get paid on none of them.

Friday and Saturday, September 31 and October 1
Friday and Saturday I am drunk. Pointless conversations with lots of people I know and don't know. I picked up a girl who

talked in non-stop poetry and was a maniac. She bit my neck. It left a bruise. She scratched my chest with her finger nails. I played Radiohead and she said that made her happy. She had red hair, and nice tits that I licked and sucked on. I pulled off her pants. "Do you have a condom?" Yes I did and I was just about to put it in and she said, "Really, I don't feel like penetration tonight."

"Please," I said, easing back.

"Fucking go then. All you care about is sex!"

"Get the fuck out," I told her. I slammed the door behind her. I wish I was nicer to her. But I am no masochist and I don't think we could've of really been friends. It would have been fun to fuck her though.

Sunday Oct. 2nd
I woke up at about 7 pm. I didn't feel hung over. I was in a good mood. Coffee. Laundry. I was not going to drink. In the laundromat a horrible panic hit my

head. I couldn't stand still. My heart was pounding. I was short of breath. I kept passing back and forth. I went home. Laundry was done. It kept on intensifying. I asked the girl downstairs to call an ambulance. My arms were starting to go numb. I don't want a heart attack. I have never gotten this bad before I thought. I kept coughing. I was breathing really fast. My hands were completely numb now. I had pains in my chest. The ambulance worker put an oxygen mask on me. He told me to try to breathe slowly.

"You do coke?" he asked

"No," I said, and the ambulance worker smirked.

"How much did you do?"

"I did some seeds, I did…"

But the paramedic cut me off.

"Don't try to talk. Breathe slowly."

They gave me something at the hospital to slow my heart rate. They ran tests. There was no coke in my system; but there were a lot of methamphetamines. The doctor told me that's why my whole body felt numb, why I was so scared, and that yes, I could have had a heart attack, I coulda been another dead-at-25.

PEOPLE ARE HAVING A BAD TIME

ON THE STREET at the corner, and on top of a turned-over mailbox stands Charles. He is in his ripped-up half a shirt. He thinks this is a cool shirt and I think it is a stupid and dumb shirt. But whatever. We are going to this thing tonight whether he looks like a dick or not. It is okay because I will most likely act like a dick, that being my nature.

"Charles, how are things, man? I see that your dressed up nice."

"What? Oh, the shirt. I love this shirt."

"Isn't that the shirt you got in the big ass fight?

There are still bloodstains all over it. That is kind of anti-social in a way, don't you think?" I hated talking down to him like that but it had to be done. Charles was a bit of a weird guy with his big fat lips and shaved misshapen head.

"Anti-social? What do you mean? That is what I am all about. Tom, you know that. Fuck the system, right? They fuck up, not me."

Err, fucking dumb ass. It is so easy to say the reason you do anything bad is because the world is fucked up. Let's see him try and change it. That is why we were going to this seminar for this charity group. You see the commercials on TV. They advertise that the seminars have free tofu. I understand them wanting to give that shit away.

It pissed me off the most because I was wearing a suit jacket and my best pair of jeans. I wanted to impress the good people. I wanted to get invited to their humus and red wine party afterwards, and I was worried that Charles was going to ruin it. We had decided to go to the thing after eating McDonald's. We ran into a sweet looking girl in black rimmed glasses and wool knee socks outside the McD's. She screamed at us and told us about how they cut down the rain forest to have more room for cattle to graze .The main thing though was she was cute so I pretended, no, I cared about what she said, although I think we may owe these cows that we domesticated; it is impossible for them to live on their own now. We owed them at least a decent place to graze. But I took a meeting brochure anyway and Charles and I made plans to go to it. Finally do something about what was wrong with the world instead of just bitching about it. It didn't help that I had been reading some extremely left-wing literature of late.

Anyway, we got to the seminar. People were smoking outside due to the level of methane indoors because of all the soy bean and other beans and rotten pale vegetarian stomachs.

"How does it work? I am sure you all want to know." It was the girl from outside of McDonalds.

"We need your money. I know, I know, you're saying 'well I am a student. I can't help,' but I say 'fuck you...'"

Everyone gasped. People were throwing their Rastafarian hats at the stage. The crowd was getting sweaty sock smell due to all of the wool socks getting sweated out.

"We have to drop our standard of living. If you think you have it bad as a student. I suggest you go live in a hut in Africa and have your parents die when you're seven years old and be brought up by your AIDS-infected older brother. All the fucking education in the world is not going to do anything to help that!"

This was not what I expected. I had brought about twenty bucks in change and old pennies to throw into a jar. I thought it was going to be more of a gesture thing, you know, kind of like saying, "I care but I've got to live my life." This word empathy: I guess I only had a rudimentary grasp of. This girl wanted us to give up our dreams so that the world could be equal to start and then we could start getting education again, but the crowd was not for it.

They all left, or most of them. Me and Charles stood at the table eating humus and olives. Charles suggested that maybe we send this to Africa and got some mean angry glares from smelly straggly haired guys with black rimmed glasses that were wearing women's shirts that said sexy. And their girlfriends had hairy armpits and dirty hair. We got scared and left.

"Maybe some other time," I said to Charles, "when I have a bit more myself. I can hardly stay afloat myself right now. I think that girl was a bit of a fanatic."

"She seemed a little bossy," he said.

Strong or independent, that is what I saw when I first saw her. She was trying to make a difference. "Sure was." I said with a chuckle. But she was right. She was right, but who the fuck is really willing to give up that much? Not that many, that's for sure. Not me, I'm sorry to say. Not now at least.

CONTROLLED WRITER

I RAN INTO JULIANNE on the street. I saluted her with my hot dog. She is a vegetarian. I had asked her out the day before at work and was turned down. I walked home and got an OE and ran into Andy.

"You alright man?" he asked, reading the nightmare of rejection on my face.

"No. I got shot down by that girl at work."

"That sucks. I've been really stressed myself lately," he said, producing a prescription bottle from his pocket.

"What's that, Andy?"

"Benzodiazepine."

"Nice."

Andy and I have spoken about benzos before. For months I was on Ativan after a heavy drinking binge last year.

"It's okay," he says.

I offered him a smoke. My OE was hidden in my coat.

"I got something for the stress too. Christmas time, you know?"

He shook his head. Evidently he did and does know what I meant.

"Well, you want to come over?" I asked him. We were a block away from my house. He did. I put on some TV and told Andy he could make some bacon and eggs if he was hungry. He asked me several times if I was sure.

"YES!" I told him. "Don't worry."

He proceeded to ask questions about how to cook them: what temperature did I cook eggs at? And then the same for bacon and if he could use some toilet paper to soak up the fat from it.

"Have you taken those pills yet today

Andy? You seem pretty out of it," I asked, swilling the OE. It was twelve o'clock and I felt real low class. I told Andy that he should eat at the table. He had sat down on my bed to eat.

"People are fucking idiots Andy. Fuck! Some guy at work says that Henry Miller is misogynous. Or like a lot of artists that are misogynous, or at least called misogynous. I don't hate women. I don't think I hate women. I don't want to be a woman-hater."

"Maybe it is something out of your control?" murmured Andy.

"Andy, I don't buy that shit. I can control it! That's what being human is all about, CONTROL!" And I finished off my bottle.

"Look Tom, let's go downtown where people are."

"Fuck Andy, okay, but we have to hit the LC first."

We trudged up Gorge Road. We spoke about how Victorians have no idea how to deal with snow. I call Victorians 'cunts' several times. We get to the LC and I buy another 40 oz. of OE.

"You know, Andy, I told myself I wasn't going to drink. But then I saw that girl and I just felt my chest tighten up. I had to drink man."

"I know the feeling," said Andy.

Walking down Blanchard towards downtown we stop off at a parkade to drink. I take a piss on some needles that the junkies have left out for us and the kids. We go to the top level to drink.

"I always get a weird nostalgic feeling drinking in parking lots. I am almost twenty-five you know? I got to act my age. I got to let go of some of this shit I'm holding on to. I got to forget about all this adolescent crap, you know?"

We sit against a wall and drink from the bottle. Andy pops the pills he got from his shrink.

"This would make a great scene in a movie, you know? Fuck man, I got so much in me. I think I'm a genius sometimes and other times I think I'm a worthless shit. Confidence is the key man, you know? All those famous fucks like Christina Aguilera and Justin Timberlake and Leonardo DiCaprio – they're my age.

Fuck, and they're living, man!"

"Money doesn't buy you happiness. I know a lot of rich people that throw their lives away on booze and drugs."

"Yeah, but they got the money to go to rehab every two months if they want. Keith Richards gets his blood changed every six months, man! Money affords comforts; comforts afford happiness."

There was a pause in the conversation and I got up and went over to a snow bank and started to pitch snow balls at the wall.

"I was never good at baseball, Andy," I said, thinking the confession profound.

"Yeah, me neither," said Andy, packing a snow ball and winding up... The pitch! People knocking them out of the park on our weak-ass malnutrition arms and all.

"I get so depressed..." he added, going back to the bottle.

"You have the luxury of being depressed. You have to do something with your time. People in Africa are never depressed, because they are always looking for their next meal."

"Drunken words of wisdom," said

Andy.

We walked from the parking lot downtown to the library where we sat and checked emails and I sent a short story, a flash fiction piece of mine. I said 'FLASH FICTION' seven or eight times really loud so the girl behind us could hear. She looked like an art student. From there Andy tried to leave for bickrum yoga, his only saving grace, but I steal a bottle of whiskey and we go down to the waterfront and rap badly for hours until the security guards come and run us off. I tried to steal a bottle of wine and ended up with an assault charge and a resisting charge... I spent the night in jail. One of the conditions of my release is that now I am not allowed to associate with Andy.

CHIRSTMAS DAY IS WONDERFUL

I'M SITTING ON MY BED in a hoodie and boxers, crying like a baby, thinking "Why do I hold on to hope? Why do I need this fucking hope when all logic points to doom? This is what makes things hurt so bad, when what I know is going to hurt happens. This 'oh no, not this time, this time it will be different' jazz."

I have lost all hope for what I cared for at one time in my life. I was on the streets and drinking every day. I walked around yelling at people and giving cops the finger. I begged for spare change.

My thing was to do it really fast like an auctioneer. But then a girl came along and hope started to creep back into my life. With girls I always wanted it to last forever. I always tell myself that they want me more than I want them, that I am in control. This is my hope, but it's never the case and as much as they tell me that they are worried about me fucking other girls and that they love me... Well, it must all be lies. In my case, at least...

So, right now, like I said, I am on my bed in the rooming house, writing on the laptop I bought. And hell, shit, I was crying because a girl I went out with in high school who sent me an email wishing me a merry Christmas did not answer an email from me (well, three emails), so I sent a fourth email saying that I was sorry that I sent three emails and that it was only because I thought she was still in love with me and that I was a loser. I was also coming down off the coke.

My next door neighbor is a ninety year-old man and coughs all the time. My room is across the hall from the washroom and he just went to the washroom. I know it was him because I heard his trademark fart and piss piss piss in the toilet and on the toilet seat. He doesn't close the door so I can hear it loud and clear, but hell, the old guy is probably just afraid that he'll fall down in the washroom. It's good of him. I can't wait until the day I wake up and go for the morning piss and I find him there, pants around his ankle, and his old dead cock hanging flaccid on the floor of the washroom. So I am a little on the emotional side lately. The girl that pulled me out of my drunken street nirvana later dumped me, against my hopes and wishes. I was with her for a year. It was a messy break up, mostly my fault, but she didn't have to be such a bitch about it. I might go into more detail about that, or I might not. I hope not. Moving on...

It is the 30th of December, I think, right now. It is four in the morning and I don't think I am going to sleep tonight, and that is by choice because I have Ativan which could put me to sleep pretty well. But I was thinking about all this self pity and shit. Fuck, what am I looking for? Someone to save me? YES! I want someone to come along and think I am the hottest thing since the 'Hot oven 3000.' Rick Thomas is doing a show on it on one of the late night programs I watch when I get bored of porn. But shit, again, still that hope that someone is going to save me. The saved don't look like they are having all too interesting lives though. All they really talk about is how good it is to be saved and smile phony looking smiles and drink lemon-aid. Some people say they are always learning, but talking to my ninety year old neighbour tells me different. All the fuck he ever talks about is how he worked so hard and how hard done by he is. Mind you, maybe he isn't saved. He is in a rooming house with a shared bathroom and kitchen in Montreal at ninety. Well, I got a nice glimpse of my future...

So, I am thinking now if that pathetic email to that girl is going to get a reply. (Oh hopes!) It was quite depressing, and poorly written. I think I ended it with: Fuck!

fuck fuck fuck
sorry
bye ____

HER NAME IS NOT ____

HER NAME IS NOT ____. I just don't want to use her name. Why? Because I don't and that should be enough... Anyway it could get a response, but what will it be? That damn hope keeps me up at night sometimes. But fuck, it's pathetic, really, that I get all hoped out of shape because of what amounts to a Christmas card in this day and age. She was probably thinking: "This is what I get for being a nice person? A bunch of fucked up emails about weird shit that is misspelled and follows absolutely no normal or sensible path, without linear thoughts or themes, a lame attempt of seduction through text?

Does he not get that I haven't answered the last three emails? Why does he think, Oh god, that I'm such a good person and that he cares about me really but it was just an email to see how he was doing...? Sorry about your ex-girlfriend, but man I haven't seen this guy for two or three years. What the fuck is he on?"

Coke or Ativan, I would say, if that question were posed. Due to the ulcer I got on December 24th, I cannot drink any alcohol. Oh and that was a trip, the ulcer, sitting in the emergency room at the hospital because I honestly thought my stomach was going to burst open... And even with the worrisome thoughts that my stomach would burst I still managed to try and make eyes at a girl in the emergency and who the fuck knows what she was going through? Certainly something worse than an ulcer. I felt bad about it as soon as I thought 'nice ass' as she walked by. I waited there. They took x-rays and again in my gown, ass showing, I gave a little smile to the x-ray operator. What a little weasel they must think of me down at the hospital. Anyway, I got the medication and shit, the Ativan, but the coke is a prescription I wrote myself.

Oh hope. It is what keeps those bums with shit-stained pants and white beards alive and the Queen of England in dresses. It is what keeps William Shatner (in his case, money, but I am sure he still wants to be a real actor) acting. Bag ladies. Such Hope! Your luck is going to change! But in all likelihood, it will not because why are you special? Why should your life be any better? At least you were not born in Africa or Siberia or China, or just about any country in the world not in the West. The fact that this is funny is because it is so petty. What the fuck would some poor African think reading this? Free health care? Access to health care, the luxury of depression and inaction, and how long will that last?

It is not like I haven't had these talks with myself before. I am developing multiple personalities with this shit. My favourite is the little kid that just wants what he wants although the other people in the world are getting less and less sympathetic with him. "Go do something for it then," they say. And I go back to the mud puddle and roll around a bit more and make some mud pies and dance around in my PJ's and eat peanut butter and jam sandwiches and look at dinosaur books and laugh at fat people. Kid stuff, you know? So it is four o'clock and one of those Ativans is looking pretty inviting right now. Take one with water and forget this brain fart. Because I am an American and I have a dream of procrastination and doing very little for the so very much I have and you know what? I know how this sounds and I hate what I am, in a way, but hope keeps me in constant wait. Hope. Fuck they should bottle the stuff, and sell it, but then that would solve nothing, globally speaking.

Money is hope... Reality is depressing... Self loathing is stupid... Themes are hard to keep running... Drugs numb swirling minds... Nothing changes with time... Life is a sphere... Life is too complex for the human mind... Life is made up of contradicting truths... Thought isn't food...

OUT OF PLACE IN COMFORTABLE SITUATIONS

Always out of place in comfortable situations
Side of the road dreams
The sad light of dreams
Cause what do they mean
Dreams

Road dust on your legs
You've been running
You've become a slave
In the sad lights sleeve
Just blowin off steam
Just blowin off steam

I LET JACK SLEEP on my couch. His place was a sad place to live. It made me feel bad for him, for his liver. Sometimes in the middle of sex with Sally I'd think of Jack in his shady sad hotel drinking by himself (very unattractive scene) to keep from cumin.

We were both transients in Montreal when I met him in a homeless shelter. I had just arrived from Halifax and had no money after drinking it all up the first night and I was reading some beat generation book dreaming about being a part of it and I noticed a tall guy (Jack) in the corner of the homeless shelter reading a book by Mordecai Richler I had read. He looked up and he had some soulful eyes. Not the dead embittered eyes of most of the others that were at the homeless shelter. I walked up to him and called him a writer. He said yes. He's a couple years younger than me. He was soulful then. I have his notebooks. I am reading them over.

In Regina, Jack slept on the side of the dirty highway the first night. Jack says there was a nice bush there where he'd hide his belongings and a cold beer store not two blocks away.

In the morning's hot sun Jack would lay all his shit out on the grass without shame. He was concentrating on relaxing.

A guy came up to Jack on a bike. He had a salon-done Mohawk. The guy held up his beer. "Cheers for beers," he said. Then he slowed down and turned back towards Jack and sat down with him. "Mind if I have a beer with ya?" he asked.

"Sure," Jack said. Anyone can have a beer with Jack.

"What you do here?" Jack asked the guy after a pause.

"Well my name is Digby." Digby was probably a latent homosexual according to Jack. "I work with the parks. It's nice to be around all the nature."

Jack thought about nature and about what it really meant. He remembered a huge truck stop just outside on Winnipeg around where those bizarre decapitations happened on a grey hound bus. The truck stop was surrounded by muddy fields. A smell of gasoline. Jack remembered saying to himself, "Ah! The great outdoors..."

"Digby, nature is especially good

when it is surrounded by city. Hopefully if we play our cards right, sooner or later we'll have no nature not surrounded by city..."

Jack snickered and brushed back his own Mohawk he had at the time—a checkerboard shaved in the side.

"You ever read Chuck Palahniuk?" Digby asked him.

"Yes, I have."

Jack remembers he said this with enthusiasm—which happens when you find someone that is not just another tabloid following peon. No, they that read fiction that is in popular demand. "What makes you ask?" Jack asked Digby.

Digby looked Jack in the eyes and tried to hold back a laugh that Jack suspected would have been girlish... "You just seem so free... Like you can do anything. I see a lot of hitchhikers come through here that have these really tough attitudes, Jack wrote. He knew these types and disliked them but always tried to come up with theories that would justify the asshole-ish demeanour.

"Digby, you got a beer for me?"

Digby then handed Jack a beer.

"Cheers for beers man!" Digby then said.

"For sure," Jack answered and cracked open the beer. "Hey Digby what I said about nature being surrounded by city might come true but I don't like it too much…"

Digby looked up into the clear blue sky and with his finely-cropped Mohawk—Jack notes that the image made him slightly sad—that the world could marginalize something then market it to the new badly dressed yuppie hipsters.

"Let's go down town and drink in a park. Are there some hot punks in town?" Jack said.

Digby got a huge 'hey you guys' smile on his face. "Yeah they hang out at the park. I don't talk to them. They're crazy…"

"What makes them crazy?" Jack asked—patiently.

"I got my bike," Digby said.

"Well I have all my worldly possessions in this duffel bag."

Jack gets up and carries his huge

duffel bag to the bushes, kicking it a couple times.

Then Jack took Digby's bike and hid it in there, too. He crossed the street followed by Digby.

"Nah," Digby said as Jack puts it 'as if a dishwasher avoiding the old bacon stretcher joke'.

"You got work tomorrow?" Jack wanted to know.

"No," said Digby.

"What's the problem then?" Jack wanted to know.

Jack notes that Digby's voice changed from a 'cool' voice to a 'Jehovah witness voice when a point of fact that disproves his faith has been uttered'

"It's my father's bike," says Digby.

"Is your father dead?"

"No."

"Well, he has a shitty bike and no one will steal it," Jack said and continued walking towards the downtown leaving Digby...

JACK WENT DOWN to the park after Digby

had bitched out.   Jack sat down among the punks.

"What's up?" Jack asked the crowd.

"Party," answered an indescribable person.

"Sounds good," our hero conceded with beer in hand.

There were about twenty of the crew at the park that day. Half were natives in their 30's with jail tatts all over their bodies. Seventeen to twenty-five year old white kids made up the other half.

Jack sat in a part of the park called 'the spot' which reminds me of the names my little crew of misfits gave drinking spots back home.

Hitch-hiking Jack had been talking about *four-directions* (to stoned truck drivers mainly) how this simple chain—diagram had been found in five or six different aboriginal people's tribes across the world who had no connection. Jack ventured to ask one of the natives with jail tatts about this.

"What the fuck does it matter what it means? Look who's here. White, black, native, Indian and whatever *you* are…"

People were laughing and Jack felt like he had said something 'unspeakable' which I understand and maybe he did, however I doubt he meant it that way.

"I think it's beautiful. What I heard about the four directions was that it predicts a time when the races of the world unite. My mother read me native myths each night before bed. I got mad respect man."

The biggest meanest looking guy stood up and said, "We are all of the same earth!"

Jack replied, offering, "You want a beer man?" I'm sure it was a touching moment.

JACK WAS MAKING EYES at a girl who instantly made him think of Joni Mitchell. She had a soft smile and it was hard for Jack not to be captivated—something about her was special to Jack.

"I am going to buy a 24!" Jack announced to everyone.

Then Jack went up to the girl and

asked if she knew where the beer store was, and if she could show him where it was.

"Of course I can and listen if you would like to come over to my house after and we can have a bottle of wine I have there. That'd be cool."

Jack asked if they could listen to Radiohead, too. For some reason Jack thought that was a sweet thing to ask her, and that she knew it.

"Of course," she answered visibly glowing.

They doubled on her bike, down the street to the beer store. They doubled as far as they could but they were both drunk and that made it short-lived. They slammed the bike against the beer store window and Jack went it and demanded a twenty-four of beer which was fifty-six bucks that Jack reluctantly paid.

Jack and the girl put the beer in the basket of the girl's bike and walked down a wonderful quiet street, with wood fences and the occasional kid throwing a stick. Or a dog pissing on a tree. Smiling Jack wrote that they got to her house smiling like a loving couple staring into each other's face.

"It's so nice," Jack said. "Why wouldn't you want to stay?"

"I don't," she said. "I'm moving to Toronto for art school."

"Toronto sucks."

"Have you ever been there?"

"No," Jack answered.

They shared a laugh standing in front of the two-storey house.

"How do you afford it?"

"My sister and I stay here. Our father pays for it."

"That's nice of him. Does he live here, too?"

"No. He's an asshole drunk."

"At least he pays for your house," Jack said pleadingly.

"He raped me when I was a four year-old child."

"Where does he live?"

"He pays for everything. My sister and I need him before we can leave."

Inside, the art on the walls was done with light strokes and bright colors. Deep purples rivered around like the sickness of beauty, Jack notes.

"You can't have beauty without sickness. Without dark there is no light," she told Jack.

"I need a beer. I have beer, but if I keep going on about deep shit like that I will sound like a hippie."

"I thought you were a hippie," the Joni Mitchell said to Jack's dismay.

Jack cracks a beer.

"I want to show you something," she then tells him. She takes Jack by hand up to the roof and they sit and drink beer and hold each other's hand and Jack shouts at her neighbors.

"I hope you don't mind waiting for my friends to come over," she asked Jack. Then the door bell rang...

Her friends didn't like Jack; at least he got that impression while he was doing a drunken Elvis impression with (Joni's) her guitar.

Her friend, who Jack refers to as 'Bull dyke', said Jack played the guitar like he was trying to rape it.

"Why not let *her* play?" said 'Bull dyke'.

Jack handed the girl the guitar and she played some hippie-esque song. 'Bull dyke' seemed appalled by something. She didn't say anything but Jack got an unsettling aura from her.

Then they all went off to the party.

JACK WAKES UP AFTER BLACKING OUT at the party. He is rolled up in a carpet. It is 6 am and everyone is on acid. He leaves after asking what had happened, which everyone finds hilarious. He takes a cab to where he stowed his shit.

JACK WAS IN THE STAIRWELL drinking with Buffy a native girl who had 'Vulgar' tattooed across her chest... Anne a crazy, depressed girl who was always on some drug and Steve, a reserved guy that at the moment was being chewed into by his woman. Steve held the phone a couple inches from his ear while his screaming girl bellowed out of the phone: "You FUCKER! ASSHOLE! BITCH!!!"

"What?" Steve asks in a small voice and explains to her where we are and hangs up and returns his cell to his pocket. "She's going to be joining us soon," he says.

Anne asked us all what we thought about euthanasia, and Steve said there was a lot of them and they all hardy-har about it. Anne had done an essay about it in school and she thought it should be allowed. It was decided that no one really cared either way.

Then they all talked about the injustice of the wars in Afghanistan and Iraq.

Steve's girlfriend who Jack thought looked like Patty from Charlie Brown showed up and Jack showed everyone the little book he had gotten from an Esso station washroom that was entitled 'Sexual Positions from Around the World'. Steve and his girlfriend started dry humping and the rest of them left them and went out to Buffy's car.

THE PLAN WAS TO GO out to the side of the highway and fly a sign and get as much beer as possible. Buffy's car was an old boat and they drove to a good place. Jack and Anne and Buffy, they held up a sign that Jack and Anne had drawn up––made pop references on it and TV personalities exclaiming to give money and they made about 160 bucks in the end just holding a sign that read 'Oprah would spare some change' in drunken script with obese rolled figures drawn in magic marker.

They got a 24 and went down to Jack's camp. The bugs were out. It was dark.

"Hey! Let's drive the car around and drink," Jack suggested.

"Good old drinking and drivin'," Buffy said, and off they went. Buffy is a mad driver doing doughnuts in the park in the center of the town.

"Fuck yeah!" Jack screams holding beer out the window. "This is art!" Jack brags about his irresponsibility. Fuck Jack.

YOU'D BETTER F**CKING TIP

IDIOTS SCREAM IN THE STREET. I've promised myself-her that I would not drink. It's around midterms and she is studying late. She studies at school because I am too much to be around while she is trying to study.

I catch the train downtown and go to a strip club. There is a guy in a nice suit at the door and he asks for five bucks which I hand over. He looks like he wants to slap me because I don't tip him.

I suspect she's cheating on me. I have been doing coke a lot behind her back. It helps me deal with it all.

The strip club is dimly lit and lap

dances are ten bucks. Two beers are seven-fifty. I attempt not to tip the semi-attractive bartender. She says, "You better fucking tip," so I do. Her tits are big but sag. I get the feeling that she used to be a stripper. I can see the man in the suit going up to her one day after closing time saying something like, 'You're beautiful, but it's time to bartend.'

A voice: "Hey guys, put your hands together for big titty TINA HEEEEEY!"

Tina is a fake blond with high white boots and when she smiles you can see uneven yellow, almost brown, teeth.

Jack's in the perv seats up by the stage. When I get down on my luck it feels good to be with a comical guy like Jack. Sure, she was cheating on me. But I cheated on her. Jack hadn't fucked a girl since that fat, native girl—after he wrapped her car around a street lamp post. They fucked in some bushes. He left the next day.

I tell Jack that I got to go piss.

Jack grabs my collar and pulls me closer to his BO and bad breath—stale cigs...

"You got blow?"

I brush him off. "I gotta piss man."

On stage, Tina bends over in front of some old sweaty, bald man. She pulls her ass cheeks open and the old man throws toonies at her crack trying to get them in her... She turns and her angry face changes to a smile when she realizes it's an old bald man. I get the gag reflex....

The washroom smells like piss, more so then most washrooms. The lights flicker in seizure-inducing intermittence. I wash my hands and go in to the stall and do a line off the toilet paper dispenser. As my head flies back from the line I feel nothing—then horny.

I go out and Jack is next to the old man, jaw wide open, gaping at Tina fucking imaginary cock on the filthy stage covered in sick-looking stains. I walk out into the rain and leave Jack, but thinking about what he had written about the day he left Regina.

JACK SAYS THE GUY ACROSS THE MEDIAN, was looking at him, as though he wanted to say something to him. Jack knew the look; Jack knew that this feeble looking guy on a bike would chime up to speak to him.

"You won't make money," said the man indicating Jack's sign that read 'broke and hungry anything helps'—Jack knew that was shit. Jack had made fifty bucks in an hour before the feeble man showed up.

"Thanks for the tip," Jack says, trying not to make eye contact.

"I know where you can get a bike."

Jack thought he could use a bike.

"I have no money for a bike," Jack told him.

"I am a security guard at…" the guy told Jack the name of a company that Jack instantly forgot. "The bike has been sitting there for about a week unlocked, and in Regina that means it's fair game."

So they walked a couple blocks up to get the bike. On the way they ran into Steve's girlfriend. She was short for a pack of smokes and Jack offered to split a pack, which she thought was a good idea, and after they all went back to Steve's backyard where the weird security guard wanted to read everyone's tarot card. Jack asked if he'd be a famous writer some day. It wasn't in the cards.... Also the tarot card read suggested that Jack's life might not have much life left to live.

Jack rode the bike down to the High was and was picked up instantly.

When she gets in she puts her arms around me. And I turn the computer off and I take out my floppy disk.

We have a good fuck and then watch The Daily Show. Then we go to bed. I wonder in the dark what Jack is up to in the night. I kiss Sally's sleeping forehead and slip into slumber.

ARGUMENTS

Money, I do not have
I see them on the street
I see me
I see them sleeping in doorways
Eyes seem far away
Romanticizes me
Love me
And they gave up on that
It's gone down
Away
Forever

SALLY WAKES ME UP in the morning. She

has found a matchbook in my pants pocket that has the strip club's name on it.

"I told you I didn't want you to do my fucking laundry. You got to chill the fuck out."

This is the wrong tact. But it's all the wrong tact.

"What's the name of this place? Golden Girls??? Who the fuck are you? What the fuck?"

She is pissed.

"Look Jack was lonely."

"Jack Dingle? What kind of name is that? How do you know him? What the fuck? Who are you?"

"You know who I am. Look, I didn't even stay that long. I found it kind of gross..."

"I have to get to class," she says. "Try not to sit on your ass all day." She gives me a kiss and storms out of the room, which seems funny to me.

The argument would continue. About an hour later the phone rang. I knew it was Jack and I didn't answer. As much as I knew the guy was sweet deep down, he's only as much as he acts and lately that's pretty despicable.

I get up and pull the sheets back on the bed and stretch out my arms. I am lucky to have Sally. I really hope she is not fucking around on me. It is not so much that she'd be fucking around that would hurt as much as me not fucking around on her. Somehow that feels like she's emasculating me in some way. She keeps the house nice and has taught me a few things about cleanliness and general happiness. The phone rings again. I know it is Jack. Jack does not get this thing about leaving me alone for one fucking day. The phone keeps ringing. We have no answering machine. Twelve rings. I go to the washroom and wash my face. Thirty fucking rings and I pick the damn phone up.

"Hello?"

"Hey man! It's Jack…"

"Hey. I was just at the coffee shop. Just ran in, right in time I guess."

"Yeah I tried to call a couple times, I think."

"Oh, sorry."

"What you up to?"

"Just relaxing you know?" I don't think Jack knows what relaxing means. You know 'dealing with himself'. Jack's fucking needy as fuck.

"Yeah yeah so let's go do something…"

"Ah.."

"Look man, I need to talk to you."

"What about?"

"Ah, kinda would like to talk to you in person."

"What is it?"

"Can I borrow like twenty, forty bucks?"

"Ah!"

"This girl is in town."

"Who?"

"This girl…"

"Fine man."

"I'll be by in an hour."

Jack hangs up the phone.

The key is in the door and it opens. It's Sally. She looks like she's been crying.

"What? Has it been raining?"

Sally looks at me with contempt. "Yeah. But I am a little upset…"

"What? Are you failing or

something?"

Sally goes down to her knees and starts sobbing. I throw a pillow at her for comfort. I think better of my tact and walk over to her and put my hand on her head and kiss her neck. "You're wonderful babe," I whisper in her ear. "I'm sorry."

"I know," she says and pulls away from me. "I cheated."

I stand up and walk over to the liquor cabinet and grab a bottle of whiskey. A knock comes on the door. It's Jack. Sally has answered and I can hear her saying, "It's a bad time."

"Let him in!" I yell.

"Okay. Come on in Jack."

"What's wrong Sally?" says Jack.

"Nothing..." Sally answers, wiping her tears.

"I just need to borrow that money," Jack says.

I throw the money at Jack. Then I throw another fifty at him.

"What the fuck?!" Jack says. "That girl from the club last night. I went home with her man!"

"Perfect Jack. I am sure you and her have a lot in common," Sally said.

"Now now... I am happy for you Jack—she seemed like a nice girl."

"She is coming over in an hour or two."

"Jack this is my home, I don't know if I want a ho in here."

"Not a ho, a stripper."

"What's the difference?" Sally says.

"I am sure she's love answering that question honey. Look we are taking a break, I am taking a vacation for a week, I'm gonna go down to Montreal—you game Jack?"

Jack looks around for a cup and then pours a yellow juice cup full of whiskey and takes a drink.

"What the fuck...? It's not a bad idea," Sally says in a hopeful, civil tone.

"Okay, I got the tickets last night."

Jack excuses himself and goes out the door with his money.

"Call around five," I yell after Jack. "We need to catch a flight at nine."

Jack says, "Will do," and shuts the door.

"Are we broken up?" I ask Sally.

"I care about you."

"You slept around..."

"Yeah."

"Was he better?" I asked.

"He and his friend kept me cumin for hours."

Two guys hey? She had a train run on her. A table separated us which I picked up and smashed and then started kicking till it was pulverized into splinters of wood while Sally looked on apathetically.

"Some time apart would be a good thing for both of us."

I gave Sally a kiss and walked out.

In Montreal

Run away with me
See what we'll find

THE MEALS ARE MUCH BETTER IN FIRST CLASS. The three of us were treated like kings; well Tina was treated like a queen. She looked very sweet when she wasn't in stripping gear. Jack had asked her to come along, told her that there were ten times better strip clubs in Montreal. We were served Champagne complimentary. And I tried my best not to think of the indifferent expression on Sally's face when

I shut the door. We were on our way to Montreal in the middle of the night in the middle of the winter.

JACK WAS READING a copy of "Less Than Zero" and Tina read a Time magazine. I stared out the window. I dreamed that this would be something. I dreamed that everything else was life and that these times, these spontaneous things that carefree people do are the only things that one can do if they want to ever be in heaven because there is nothing else but this...

We got to the snowy door step of the hostel at six am happy to be away from our collective everythings. Free. Jack had not had a drink the whole plane ride and neither did Tina, but I didn't bother to ask why. Coke was the thing going through all our minds I guess, because after signing in and getting assigned rooms and beds and having little sleep, we all got up around 7 PM and the first thing we did was take the metro down to Berri-UQAM to get coke.

We went to a bar where Jack nursed

a Guinness the four hours we were there and Tina talked and surprised me with who she was, that she was anyone, which sounds so horrible but is the truth of how I thought of her.

"I am really happy I did this. It is such an adventure. Makes me feel nineteen again," she said.

"You couldn't be that much more than nineteen," says Jack sounding strangely charming—a side of Jack that I hadn't seen for a while.

"Really, he is right. You *are* gorgeous," I said holding her hand and kissing it.

"Charmed," she said.

"The ass that's our roomy though… God man!" Jack said referring to the gigantic Australian that snored face down in his pillow, his ass—his hemorrhoid ass— stickin' out of his torn, dirty boxers."

"Yeah fatty fat fat was fucking fat. What a fat fuck."

"He was very sweet to me," Tina said.

And I was about to ask what sweet meant to her, given her profession.

"He fucking snored. How's the girl dorm?" Jack asked.

"MM," was all Tina said.

WE TOOK TURNS going off to the wash room and snorting lines. The music was heavy in the Bar. Foufounes Electric. There was a dance floor and fueled by alcohol, I and Tina went and danced on the dance floor to alternative 90's hits. Jack sat back and looked cool smoking in the smoking area. He was talking to three punks when we got back and telling them "you see because Jack Kerouac ain't got nothing on me" and the Punks were nodding and saying, "Yeah yeah"

I noticed that Jack had given in and had two beers in his hand. "GG Allin see? He was a performance artist man, all that shit, that's punk it's all art man. I use to think art was all gay and shit, but it's all connected you know? Like you got the Velvet Underground who were influenced by Bob Dylan and Kerouac who influenced Bob and the Velvet and then you got Keroauc's friend who did spoken word with Kurt Kobain who is a poet man!"

Jack likes to get into these one sided conversations. They make sense in a way.

Jack and Tina went off somewhere and I lost them. I walked around Montreal at night. Wind-swept street-snow drifts and all, but there still was an insane amount of people walking around. I ran into a girl with red hair and asked her to come have a beer. "Sure," she said and leaned into me for warmth and we stepped into the closest hole in the wall bar.

"What's your name?"

"Eloise. I go to McGill."

"Oh, I'm Tom. I'm from Halifax but I use to live here. I love it here."

"Halifax! I love Halifax, it's a beautiful place."

"Yeah."

Then we sipped our beers and stared into each other's eyes. The energy between us was magnetic. We just sat there and we both started laughing. "I love it when this happens." She said and I knew what she meant. Because it meant nothing, we were simply two lost souls that got blown together in the beauty of the snow swept street in Montreal one night. Leaving her home in the sunny morning I knew I'd never see her again, but that was not the point—one nights stands are holy, they are the purist form of love in the world—before the games and the doubts come to play... in that one night you are each other's god. You are each other's fantasy—the less you talk the better it is.

I WOKE UP IN THE HOSTEL around five pm and took a shower. I put on a pair of jeans and a T-shirt and went to sit down in the main area of the hostel where people mingled. Jack was sitting there with an annoyed snicker on his lips. Four or five people were in the kitchen speaking French. Tina had gone out to the clubs— to look for work. I sat down next to Jack who was having a conversation with a guy named Jean-Philip who was doing Yoga on the floor in the common area. The Simpson's was on and we all occasionally chuckled. And then the Aussie Mike walked in and sat down in a spot on the couch, which had his ass indent in it. Jack was cracking a couple witless remarks that a swaggering Latino guy named Joe would laugh at and say "this guy" and point at Jack with his thumb. The fat fucking Aussie fatty switched the channel to "Two and a Half Men" to all of our dismay.

"This show is so stupid," said Jean-Philip with a French pompous air, which I have always loved.

"What? It's a funny show. I've not watched cartoons since I was five," growled the Aussie sumo wrestler with food flying from his fat face.

"At least the Simpson's is clever," said JP.

"It's fucking smart is what it is," said Jack.

"And what is this? Stupid... MEN MEN MEN MEN!" JP belted out the theme music.

No offense to Charlie Sheen but it does suck.

HOSTEL

FAT AUSSIE EVENTUALLY went out somewhere. And Jean and Jack and I sat around. JP grilled Jack a bit.

"What is it that you want in life, Jack?"

Jack said nothing. Jack had been acting somewhat strange since we got to Montreal—unusually withholding. Jack leaned back and dragged his hand trough his curly hair until his hand got caught half-way through.

JP looks like a young Christopher Walken and has a similar tone in his voice. He goes to the University of Montreal for music, and he is studying to be an opera singer. This was apparent when he sang the "Two and a Half Men" theme song, which almost brought tears to my eyes.

"What do you want Jack? Because all you have to do is believe in it man and it's yours."

JP had a very cool vibe to him. He seemed very knowledgeable, too, even though he too was living in a hostel in his hometown because his girlfriend had kicked him out.

"What you grilling him for?" I asked JP with a bit of a laugh.

"Hah-Ha!" JP had a laugh that almost sounded forced. It made you feel he was a good guy.

In from the kitchen came a girl from New York, who had come to Montreal to study "electronic" music. She was blond and an actor-playwright-musician. Her age was indeterminate. Though she was attractive you couldn't put your finger on it, but something said she was pushing forty.

"Yeah Jean, what you do? You're doing yoga in a youth hostel. What kind of authority of doing what you want are you?"

"A good one. I am happy. I have passion. I am free, I love life." Jean said slightly annoyed though trying to hide it.

"Good on ya, Jean," I said.

"Thanks," Jean said in small uncharacteristic tone.

The deep voiced French owner of the hostel was showing two beautiful blond girls into the next room. We all craned our necks.

"Wonderfully," said one. "Yes, just lovely," said the other, in these cute little English accents.

Jean got up and walked over and in a deep practiced voice said, "Welcome to Montreal." The bastard then kissed their hands. The girls giggled profusely.

TINA DIDN'T COME BACK THAT NIGHT. Jack seemed distraught while we sat down and watched 'When Harry Met Sally'—the undetermined-aged girl's pick. Jack sat right next to the blonde English girl who was wearing a shirt that really showed off her tits. Her tits were perfect. Jack hits on girls like a child would. He makes fun of them and everything to make them laugh. She was laughing a lot.

"Fuck off and just watch the movie," she said pushing on Jack chest. Jack had this telling, glowing smile when she did that.

I excused myself from them all and went to the phone in the lobby and dialed Sally's number in Vancouver. I got the machine and told her I was in Montreal and that I would try back later. I wondered where she was, but then decided I didn't really care. Things with her weren't working out really.

"We are going to the Billy Kun!" announced JP.

"The what?" asked Melissa (the undeterminably-aged women) giggling a bit at the name.

"Yeah," said Jack. "The Billy Koon."
Everyone laughed at him.

"What? That's the name of it. It's a bar."

"I'm game," I said.

The English girls said that they would go for a bit. Joe the swaggering Latino guy was up for it, as was the fat Aussie who had just gotten back and was eating a large bag of pork rinds which he was wiping the grease from on his torn black T-shirt that read 'Sex Machine'.

The bar was pretty chic. It had ostrich heads sticking out all over the place. They all pulled up chairs. Jack asked for Coke and JP heard this and said he too wasn't drinking. I saw that the two of them were talking, Jack looking at him as if he were some kind of father figure for Jack. When Jack is not drunk he is extremely shy and hardly says a word all night. He was probably upset about Tina's disappearance also. We left the Billy Koon around twelve and walked up Mont-Royal, the girls curling up to me, Jack and JP to keep from freezing in the vicious winds and we got in to a club. It was a loud dance club and we had a good time finally crawling into our bunks at around four in the morning.

WALKING DOWN THE STREET a couple days later I ran into Tina. She had not been heard from since we got to Montreal. She looked like she was doing well. She got Montreal heads to turn, which is something to say since the French are the most attractive people in the world (not an entirely true statement).

"Tina what and where have you been?"

"I got a job. I don't know. Jack was a good guy he just seemed like not the type of guy that could handle someone like me. I am not looking for anything important you know?"

"Yeah. It's probably best. Otherwise he'd just get hurt. It is easy to hurt him." I paused and looked up at her and she smiled. "You want to get a bite?"

"Sure," and we went arm and arm into the metro and down to Ben's diner on Maisonneuve. I always go to Ben's when I'm in Montreal. It is an old style diner lunch counter cafeteria thing. It feels like you are sitting down in the 50s or 60s.

"You like this place?" I asked Tina.

"It seems dirty," she said.

"It's a good place. It's been here a long time."

"Probably has rats."

She was probably right.

We had a couple of Rubens and watched the people bundled up walking by. After we were done she asked if I wanted to come by her hotel room.

"It's a lot nicer then that place that you guys are holed up in."

We took a cab down to old Montreal and walked in to an old brick building with golden doors and took an elevator to the second floor. Her room was big and had a nice big brass bed. Instantly, as the door closed, I grabbed her and pulled her close.

"Fuck me," she gasped. I threw her on the bed and pulled off my pants and shirt and shit as she did the same.

As I fucked her in a plethora of insane positions I thought about Jack and Sally. When we were done she laid on the bed and lit a smoke—both naked and covered in sweat watching CNN's political race coverage, not saying a word, barely thinking at all.

AFTER THE OBESE AUSSIE had gotten Jack to get some groceries from the *dep* the moronic Aussie's saving grace of making everyone amazing meals at the hostel was under way. Great pastas and meat sauces that he'd get all the girls staying at the place to try at which time he'd cop a feel.

An osteopath, he had given all the girls with strong stomachs full body massages. To think of the fat girth of his hairy body rubbing and pressing up against you was too much for many. Jack and I watched Melissa get done and snickered at each other.

Jack and the English girls got along decently. I could tell that he had a thing for the English girls. Always making excuses to wait up for them when they were out at clubs, which he wasn't invited to. It was sad to watch and everyone knew it and made fun of him behind his back about it, even me.

Jack had not been drinking for about a month now and I was glad and he seemed fairly happy. He even scored with an eastern European girl that came through one night. JP and him had taken them out to the Billy Kun.

Tonight the hostel was the most full that it had been for a while and everyone was drinking and getting ready to hit the bars for some festival of light that Montreal was having. It was also the English girls' last night and Jack and the fat fuck were going to go out to a sheesha bar with them for their last night.

The oaf and the two English girls and Jack caught a cab and went down to the fat fucker's fav sheesha bar. The English girls were going to a show at *Casa Del Poppolo* after the short hang with Jack and Fat-fuck and it was an unspoken understanding that Jack and fuck obese Aussie were not invited to the show with them. After a sick display of groping the English girls while Jack took their pictures the girls were off to *Casa del Poppolo* and they tried to say good bye.

"What? I bought all this beer and

sheesha and now you are splitting on us?"
fat bastard said.

"No, it's just it isn't really your scene
is all."

"What you mean I am not cool enough
to go with you there?" the fat fucker
asked with an air of insult. "It is a free
country."

Jack cowered in the corner quietly
saying to fat fuck Aussie sumu wrestler
fucker that it was emo music and they
probably wouldn't like it.

"No you are coming too mate," he
said to Jack. "Now girls, let's get a cab"

So they all got a cab after the teary eyed
English girls with running mascara due to
fatty-fats insistence agreed to encourage
Jack and fats to come along. They were
meeting the indecipherably-aged Melissa
there. It was chalk full of lesbians and
androgyny. Obese fatty looked as though
he had shit himself with fear while they
entered.

The English girls and Melissa were
talking at the door of the club and Jack
and Fat-fuck-fuck-fatty-obese-asshole-
reason-for-social-awkwardness sat down

on a couch adjacent to two obvious bull dykes and fatty offered to buy one a drink which the crabby face dyke simply glared at fat for reply meanwhile Melissa and the English girls had disappeared and Jack said to fatty-fat-fat, "Look man this is not our scene. Let's fucking go to a club that's more our style."

Jack and Fatty-fuck-fuck went to a club on St Denis that had the hot little teeny boppers in tight revealing clothing in a packed dance floor with everyone grinding up against each other to top 40 hits. Jack started drinking out of despair for the English girls that he now knew he would never have.

At the end of the night Fatty and Jack were the only ones left on the dance floor and Jack was kicking the air and yelling for no reason.

They got a cab and drove around looking for prostitutes and none were around. It was around five in the morning. They cab driver said, "Yes, I know girls," and he drove to five or six different 'hot spots'. "This is a good one I know. I go myself and girl really make you hot!" But that was a no go until they drove down to the Gay village and found two. Jack was all for going with the two girls to their house but fat-fat-fat-fucker was not too sure. He drove off in the cab leaving Jack.

Jack went back to the girls' house; they were in their panties and bras out in the middle of the street. They went in and one whore took her shirt off and started rubbing her breasts while the other sucked on Jack's cock. He had paid them eighty bucks. He blew his load in seconds due to the lack of sex for the last while and being horny all night being rubbed up against by scantily dressed women in the club.

"Hey, can I have forty back? That wasn't worth eighty." The prostitutes put a fork to his neck.

Jack cried while he walked home and on arrival was met by Fat-fat-fat-fucker who said, "You know those hoes were bros right?"

Jack replied, "No, I checked."

"Sometimes they tuck," was Fatty's reply.

Afterward Jack's usually snide indignation towards fatsies-sized to happen at which time I asked him why and that's when he told me. Jack had started drinking every day and was getting more and more insane.

It got to the point where Jack and me were the two people who had been staying at the hostel the longest out of everyone. We both had jobs telemarketing at the same place. It was a scam. And we knew it. Every Friday and Saturday night we'd go get a movie and watch it. The owner of the hostel had no problems with us. I looked after Jack's craziness. We each got our own private rooms.

TINA WOULD MEET ME once and a while. And I started to meet her friends—if you can call them that. More like associates. They were all coke dealers and I caught wind of a job for a driver that was needed to deliver some coke from Montreal to Halifax. Theo gave me a car and a couple thousand dollars for my trouble and I accepted. I told Jack about it and the last

night before we shipped off he decided
that he was going to have a good send off
at the hostel.

There was a group of students up from
California. They were kind of irritating
always talking about their thesis and all
that. Jack not having gone to university
is usually irate and irritable around these
types. But this brand of student was the
worse. They believed in "causes" not that
there is a thing wrong with being socially
and political aware and to care about these
things but to act as though you are above
other people because of the fact that you
did a class in international development
studies and know the inner workings of
African government or lack thereof, even
I find annoying.

Jack had been drinking all day and was
on his sixth or seventh forty of ten percent
beer when he sat down on the couch with
one eye half open and the other shut.
The student was babbling on about some
injustice in the world very sarcastically
in high pitched nasally whiny voices and
Jack just let loose.

"Hey I drive SUVs!" he said to a

student who was one of the crowd and had been talking loudly about the stupidity of red necks that drove SUVs.

A girl in black rim glasses piped up. "You're a fascist," she said.

"Faggot dyke whore," Jack said. I know Jack and he was just saying these things to goad these ultrasensitive carrot eaters on.

"How can you say that!" said a guy in the group coming up to Jack with a clenched fist.

"Fuck you mobster Italian."

The guy popped Jack in the nose. Jack grabbed his legs and pulled him to the ground. I ran up and pulled Jack off just as Jack was hauling back to smack the guy.

"Call the cops!" screamed a fat girl that had a perpetually smug suspicious look on her fat face.

"Calm down I got him. I will take him to bed," I told them.

"He's a fucking racist!" said the Fat girl and started smacking Jack and me in the face.

"Look!" I said, "You big-boned bitch.

Fuck off. I got him. I'm sorry."

A gasp went up from the entourage of 'save the world' university students and they all started to swarm. I had no choice but to defend myself. Jack was savagely beating on any one who came towards him. I heard a bitchy high pitch squeal: "I am calling the police!!!!!"

Jack and I started to struggle our way to the door. It opened and we toppled down the stairs on to the street. I guy jumped from the top of the stairs and landed on Jack's chest. I punched the guy in the nose and he started to cry running back up the steps blood going everywhere.

"Go around the block and wait at the *dep*!" I yelled at Jack.

I went back upstairs and tried to open the door to the common area where it all had gone down, but it was locked. I went to my room on the next level and picked up the coke and money and clothing and shit.

On the way out, I was about at the last step when I heard a bull dyke squeal: "There is one of them!" A fat cop came running towards me. I ran at him, jumped and stuck my knee in the air. It connected with his nose. Blood sprayed from the cops face and he went down on his knees and his hands went over his eyes. I stood frozen for a moment, thoughts racin' 'what the fuck am I gonna do about this' 'this is bad this is bad this is bad' the cop then started to fuck with his holstered gun, or something I did not stick around to find out what he was pulling out of his little utility belt. I ran three blocks and jumped into the Buick and then drove to collect my racist idiot friend who I really should not give a rat's ass about. We sped off.

NIGHT-RIDE

Hurl through surreal sadness

"WHAT THE FUCK DID YA DO THAT FOR!" I scream at Jack driving across the bridge out of Montreal in the snowy night. I am trying to do the speed limit but my foot is pushing out of anger. "Jack what the fuck is wrong with you?" Jack is groveling. He probably has some broken bones. We get to the other side and I stop at a strip mall with a liquor store. Jack's breathing is all fucked up. He has been drinking for days and he is not going to be very good company if he's going through withdrawals in the back seat. So I buy a couple 40s of whiskey and throw one in the back seat with him. He instantly crawls over to the bottle and opens it and sucks on it like a cub at its mom's teat.

It is back into the night going East, going home. Home is a funny thing to call it for either Jack or I. I left it when I was in my teens. Halifax. There is a strange sense of excitement that I get when I am going anywhere I haven't been for a long time regardless of the circumstances. The whining in the back seat slowly stops and Jack has roused himself with the booze and is looking straight ahead at the road. "I want to be in the front seat," he says.

We stop long enough for Jack to get in the front seat and Jack isn't smiling. He can sense the anger. "Is there any music here?" he asks.

I pass him the CD case and he flips through them. He puts on a Doors' album—I got my eyes on the road and my hands upon the wheel—Jack lays his head back on the head rest and closes his eyes. "Why you look after me man?"

I don't know the answer to this question. The cold night rushes past. The streetlights glare and run lines in my eyes. I think I am crying for some reason I don't know why, I don't care about most of those fuckers back there, Tina maybe, but I don't think that really. "Are you okay?"

"I think I may have broken a couple of ribs."

"Probably."

"You think they'll be after us?"

"I punched a cop, but I don't think they know the vehicle. I think we're okay. We're going to Halifax."

"Sweet!" Jack says with sarcasm that I am not in the mood for.

"Where else Jack?"

"I don't know. "

"Fuck you Jack. Look man why you say all that shit?"

"I didn't mean it; I was drunk. And you know how fucking pretentious those fucks were."

"Actions speak louder than words: I mean, fuck that doesn't work" I chuckled to myself. "My friend Jack the racist. That shit you said was vile and unacceptable I should stop the car right here and drop your scumbag ass in the middle of the highway! What is wrong with you? I don't want to know someone that says that kind of shit! Who the fuck are you?"

"I'm sorry," Jack says like a sucky baby sucking on a bottle, only it's a bottle of whiskey.

"In New Brunswick we can go to the emergency. You are going to have to deal with the pain cowboy style till then."

The road is ice and I have to be careful. I glance over at Jack a couple of time and sigh. "Jack you have to stop drinking."

"I know" Jack says, taking a drink of whiskey. "You got any blow?"

"The glove compartment," I say.

He takes it out and sticks his finger in and snorts a bit. "Give that here," I say, one hand on the wheel.

We cross the border to New Brunswick and when we get to Fredericton we go to a motel and get a room. I give Jack the keys and go to bed. Jack goes to the hospital.

STARFADE

THEY DIDN'T TELL ME how much coke was in the car and I didn't care. They gave me a sizable baggy of it and when I got up to Jack walking in a 4 am I took it out and we did a couple lines and we talked.

"What the fuck is this man?" Jack asks nose red and with broken rib wheeze.

"What you mean? What is it all about... oldest question in the world."

"No it isn't. It's about happiness, love."

"That's funny coming from you,

considering what you said last night. I understand that those smarmy know-it-alls got under your skin Jack, but really! Mobster Italian that is a little too much. You could get killed first of all for saying that. Second you didn't strike me as a person that would be like that."

"I'm not like that and that is why I can say it."

"Jack, that makes no fucking sense at all."

"Let's change subjects."

"Okay... What you want to do tomorrow?"

"I thought we were driving to Hali."

"Yeah. Yeah who wants to stay in New Brunswick? I guess we are driving to Hali. Jack you and I can drink a bit but I am telling you. I mean I can't stop you from doing anything but everything in your fucking life is fucked up by drinking."

"Same with you."

He is right.

"There are levels Jack."

We broke out a bottle of whisky and started drinking and were tanked by the time the sun came up. I decided around noon that it would be a good idea to buy a camcorder from Radio Shack. We drove along the highway drunk until we found a park area we could go out on and fuck around. I took the camcorder and we recorded each other doing stupid shit.

Jack beating a beer can yelling, "What you gonna do? Huh? What you gonna do?" Then starfade to Jack beating a beer can saying, "What you gonna do huh? What? Ya shit heel..." and starfade to grass starfade to a tree. There really wasn't that much out there in that field in the way of props.

Then Jack got that great idea to make interviews. He had a whole premise for a show worked out. It would be called "The Asshole Show". It would be a variety show where he'd have on famous guests and bring them out to a field in the middle of nowhere and ask them to beat a can and say "What you gonna do..." The day was fun because we were drunk.

Starfade.

It's around 4 PM and we both have hangovers and we are around the Halifax airport. We are both happy despite our severe hangovers. To go back home after years of being away is to be reborn. Though it usually turns out that you grow up to the point that you are sick with where you are born in a matter of months ...

We drive over the bridge looking down to the empty park that used to be Africville, a thriving African-American neighborhood that was beautiful despite the fact the city would not supply it with running water and was bulldozed down so that a park that no one goes to could be set up. All the black people were put into badly constructed houseing projects. The North End. I grew up in the North End. There is something about going home. I don't know what it is, but it makes you FEEL—perhaps it is just nostalgia... maybe it is something that can't be put into words.

BASH YOUR HANDS FOR WACKO

Bash your hands for wacko
Sell your soul for apathetic
Insane
Nasty

WE SIT IN THE BARTIN'S DANK, stinking basement. Nacnud gives a half smile to his friend Chay that he has a man-crush on and says in an undeniably phony voice "Wanna get your ass kicked at pool?" I look at Jack with an expression that I hope says 'who the fuck is this guy?' But Jack seems spaced out. His brother is pouring a tall boy into his open mouth and spills some on his dickies button down but doesn't seem to notice and with a stunned face opens another beer and starts drinking it back. Chay accepts the game. I look around at the Bartins shrine to kitsch—a Ché poster—a Hunter S. Thompson's picture done Andy Warhol style. A poster for the movie "The Beat Generation". Some kid's prank glasses that make your pupils look extremely big. Marilyn Monroe and James Dean sitting at the diner counter; Marlon Brando in Wild Ones; Reefer Madness, etc, etc. The table is covered with beer cans and bottles and flies are swarming and there is an ass smell in the air. Nacnud puts on an old blues album and the cracks of the pool balls break out like gas in an old folks' home or anti-fur rally.

"What you guys think of Shanika?" Jack asks.

I know who he means: the girl that came up to me out of the blue and told me that I might have met her before, and that she just had an abortion so she might look a bit under weight. "Who do you mean?" I ask.

"The girl that works at the café," Jack's brother says slurrily...

"Yeah, I think she's pretty cool."

"Yeah," I say.

"Oh yeah man, but Jack you know who's really cool? Cherokee."

"She is spoken for man," Jack says.

Jack's brother's girlfriend comes down the stairs to the basement with Cherokee and they sit down. "You guys talking about me?" Cherokee a dark-haired girl in a mini skirt and tank top asks.

"Yeah, we were saying that you were cool." Jack says. "Hey I was wondering are you Native?"

"No, my mom just thought it was a cool name."

"Are you joking?" I ask. She isn't but she wishes she was. She is a beautifucking girl but is, as Jack said, "spoken for". I met her new boyfriend at Charlie's. We stood there and stared at nothing with glazed eyes sipping whiskey sours for an hour saying nothing...

"Chris what are you doing?" Jack's brother's girlfriend asks Jack's brother.

"Sit cool babes."

"What beer is that?"

"What?" Jack's brother drunkenly scoffs.

"It's fucking twelve in the afternoon Chris."

We all get up and go over to Chris's girlfriend's house. Everyone but Jack, Nacnud and Chay who stay in the basement. Jack seems very intent on making a tower out of beer cans in the swarming flies.

We get to Amy's, Jack's brother's girlfriend's house. There is a smell of cat shit and piss on their veranda. We sit on the veranda. It's getting to be nice weather out. We listen to music and drink beer slowly and talk about what's been going on. Amy dishes out dirt on all the people that are not sitting around the porch—Cherokee is enthralled by the shit-talking. I kind of zone out—I talk to Chris, Jack's brother about Kbart and his rockabilly band.

"So you going to the Problem Shooters gig tonight?" asks Chris seeming miraculously completely sober—perhaps it was the walk over.

"Yeah. Sounds like a good time. Is Jack going?" I ask.

"I think he has to work." Ah! No wonder he stayed behind in the dank dungeonous basement. "You want to stick around and do some pre-drinking?"

"Sure thing," I say.

Chris winks at me and we walk casually down the steps to the driveway to the street and walk, Chris looking up to make sure Amy doesn't notice us leaving. She is too into the dish session she is having with Cherokee and we walk down to the beer store and buy a couple cases and walk up to the Bartin's again. Jack had gone but Kbart has arrived back from work and we sit out in the backyard as he strikes up the BBQ.

"Working on this new song," Kbart says with a smile indicating his own fondness of his talents. "I think it's really gonna get the ladies hopping."

"Hopping, eh?" I say.

"Oh yeah. You haven't been to a show yet have you?"

I say I haven't.

"I think you'll like it," Chris says after swilling on a beer, burger in hand.

WE STAY THERE until it gets dark and then walk down to Charlie's—a local club-bar. There we meet Cherokee and Amy who are drinking colored drinks. We sit at a table and drink continuously waiting for a respectable time to show up at the gig—Kbart has already gone to set up. Chris has one eye shut and is nodding off and Amy is looking at him with disgust.

"Wake up."

She smacks him and his head rolls and stays on his shoulder and he begins to drool. "I need a more classy man." Amy says and smiles at me suggestively.

"Ah, he's just a bit drunk," I say.

Cherokee laughs a cute laugh and then puts her hand up to her mouth with an expression on her face that says: "I should not of laughed'.

"He always has too much," Amy says. "At least he doesn't get like his brother. It sure is good he stopped drinking."

I agree with her and try to stop the

conversation for Jack's sake and not to bad mouth him in front of Cherokee who I get the impression may not know about Jack's asshole drunken behavior.

"You know how he gets all rude and violent…" Amy's says in her dishy way.

"Jack really? He seems so sweet," Cherokee says.

"Let s not talk about it," I break in and Amy drops it.

It comes time to mosey on down to the show and the place is packed with smelly punks. A couple of rock-a-billy pompadour guys stand smiling around the bar—the place is a jam spot for local bands. It's going out of business. There's a band up there playing this horrible mix between Red Hot Chili Peppers and the worse thing I've ever heard and it induces the gag reflex so I order a beer and get as far away from the band as possible which is hard in the small room…

Jack never showed—I get the story the next day.

JACK HAD BEEN GETTING PHONE CALLS

at work all night from two people. One was an old friend, with whom he had a strange and fucked up relationship; and the other was from the odd and most likely insane Shanika. Jack says that one of the messages that he couldn't get until after his shift washing dishes was, "Come on by my house after work you sexy fucking man..." It was Shanika. When he got off work, he raced to her house and there she was in panties and a bra at the door.

They watched TV in her room and fucked. He was very proud of himself. As this was happening I was at the gig and Steph came up to me and looked at me with these big fucking doe eyes that said I want to fuck you. I ended up getting laid that night, too.

Jack tells me in a hushed tone when we sit at the One World café. It is sunny out and I smile blinking in the sun and decide not to tell Jack about my sex life. I regret having done so, but when I found out I should of, it was all too late.

JACK WASN'T SEEN around Agricola for a while after that. Sometimes late at night he showed up at some drunken party and left shortly after. He was spending all his free time with Shanika who was becoming more and more anti-social and anorexic looking. Jack told me that she was not eating and it had to do with her Grandmother dying.

"What the fuck? It's her fucking grandmother! The women was fucking ninety or something!" he said one night at a party out back of Cherokee's house sitting on a ratty couch that she had in her back yard. After he said this Cherokee came out and drunkenly screamed for Chocolate milk. Jack was known now for drinking large jugs of chocolate milk at raging drinking parties. Cherokee got him to go get her a jug for herself and Cherokee went to lie down on the couch and passed out. I never really got to talk to Jack about the troubles he was having.

KBART AND JACK had been practicing to play some show at the One World café and the day had come up. Jack seemed very tense and confided in me and his brother that he had broken up with Shanika. We both told him that that was good because she was a crazy bat.

"I am worried about her," Jack said and picked at the guitar he was holding in his hand. He looked like a rockabilly guy that day—a curly Mohawk and a dress shirt opened to show a wifebeater. Kristen (Kbart) and him went up and played the show and Shanika showed up in the middle of it. Jack's guitar went bad.

After the gig, he sat out front just watching Shanika play with someone else's infant kid. He went around the corner with her and was having a smoke with her when some other guy came along and asked if she wanted to go smoke a joint. Knowing that this guy thought he was protecting her from Jack, Jack lost it. He threw a pop bottle against the wall. Ten minutes later Jack was sitting in the backyard of the Bartin's and we all tried to calm him down. But he got up and with a straight twitchy face, walked down to Shanika's house and knocked on the door until she called the cops. The cops hauled him off.

Everyone was just kind of like "Wow! Jack is acting pretty crazy..." It was strange, but we all went down to Charlie's and drank. Me and Steph fucked in the washroom and then went down to Steph's friend's house who was having a party around the corner, and around 2 in the morning just as a Domino's pizza showed up Jack came around the corner. He looked mad—like crazy. "I punched the wall until they let me out," he said holding up his hand we could see that is was bleeding and lumpy some of the girls drunkenly talked to him in soothing tones. I decided that this was a good time for me to leave. The next day I went to the airport and flew back to Vancouver. About three months later I got a letter from Jack—the return address was Nova Scotia's correctional facility.

Hey bud how are you? Why didn't you let me know you were going? I got together with this girl and things kinda got fucked up—they got fucked up in a fucked up situation. I won't go into details cause it hurts too much, and I have thought about it too much. But I get out next week and I am gonna go into rehab. No one speaks to me anymore. I will send you an email. Hope to hear from you.

I am in here all day... they took my freedom. I don't know if you want to hear this shit man but here... You remember Steph? I saw her. We were together for a week, and I know I know that is not really a long time. But it was intense. We stayed up all night and confessed our love to each other. You ever get that feeling like you knew someone that you knew them before you met them, Tom, man it was like that! It was like that! I am not crazy! I know people that are crazy never think they are crazy but man—this is just the truth. She is just afraid of the truth. She is afraid of getting hurt. I broke her window okay, and I cut myself a bit with some glass...

I am sorry for writing you this, but now no one cares. No one's talking to me man—and I know you will. I trust you.

Jack Dingle

I got the story with no erratic babble later. Jack was sleeping with a girl and living with her. Then she broke it off and he went and got drunk and broke into her house trying to talk to her. She asked him to leave; he wouldn't. The cops were called, and he fought the cops. I have not emailed him or spoken to him since.

LAST WORDS OF THE FORGOTTEN

YOU SEE THE GRASS EXPANDING out before you in the yard. You're tired. You have been up all night. You think about counting the blades. You walk forwards on shaky legs and think for a second where you are and your past flashes. Is this the end?

Your gut is swollen as you walk the dewy grass to the residential street and let your instinct guide you back to the main street. You glare at the man walking to work in the sunlight. Your head hits the wall of the black out the night before. You remember being in a bar with a girl you ran into from your past. You remember the smile on her face change through the course of the night, fading into a grimace back to a non-respectful smirk.

You see the ocean but have no idea which one it is... people could be speaking German or Greek for all you knew... Anyway what do you care? You jingle your pockets and you hear that coinage ding. You have a flash of a man pushing you out a door.

"You don't fucking know!" you say, you yell. You wander around looking for a place to piss.

You're told, "These people can help you."

YOU LIKE THE UNDERPASS, *your* underpass. You smile cause they don't know what you need and you'd rather be there when the bomb hits. You remember when they use to be positive, you remember.

You know the world is coming to an

end. It is the year of the hopeless. And you've written your story a million times and realize how useless your apologies have been.

You wish you never had a name. You wish you never had a care. You wish you never wasted your time on petty things that brought you pain. You never wonder if you're sane, because the end is now. The end is now.

Reality in Closing

"HE DOESN'T SEEM TO RESPOND TO ANYTHING," said the Doctor in the white coat looking at the man huddled in the corner of the room. He was standing with another man in a cowboy hat. The man in the cowboy hat tapped on the plexiglass and the sighed.

"Seems to be more and more of them," the man in the cowboy hat said.

"Can you blame them?" the doctor

asked. His lips contorted up into a weasel like smile and he fondled his breast pocket for a pen which he retrieved and clicked as the man in the cowboy hat looked annoyingly at him. The man in the cowboy hat coughed. The Doctor looked at the man in the cowboy hat and put the pen back in his pocket. "You know we're the lucky ones to have purpose. I have been studying them and with some hypnosis we can extract the lustre of a dream world that many of the social catatonics have. As brilliant as the Hollywood movies of the old days."

"Filth if you ask me," said the cowboy once again looking into the room through the plexiglass.

"For a man of your education... Martin, I am surprised," said the doctor.

"I know this one. Remember I found him on the outside.

"Yes, really remarkable this one and his, ah, coping skills. Walking that far..."

The man in the cowboy hat walked

out of the observing room leaving the doctor, who resumed clicking his pen, and walked down the corridor with the flicker of lights and the sounds of the occasional nightmares which plagued the facility. He turned into a room with the sign that read Mr. Owens and walked into a room with a fridge and a table and sat down on the bed. Mr. Owens removed his cowboy hat and looked down at the floor. The pattern of the floor had been subject to reasonless calculation by Mr. Owens. He'd count the orange squares and his mind would wonder. He was on the digressional stage of the cope.

Sand storms made being outside dangerous. Owens eyes were already damaged from the storm several years ago. What had the Doctor said about the man? 'Hollywood movies...' Martin Owen smiled and lay back on the bed... The doctor would be around soon to administer his medicine, to help him rest, to help him forget the red sky...

FIN

www.ingramcontent.com/pod-product-compliance
Lightning Source LLC
Chambersburg PA
CBHW030509260626
47157CB00005B/1710